MAGIC

A NOVEL BY

WILLIAM GOLDMAN

DELACORTE PRESS / NEW YORK

Acknowledgment

"Heartbreak Hotel," words and
music by Mae Boren Axton, Tommy
Durden and Elvis Presley. © 1956
by Tree Publishing Co., Inc. Reprinted
by permission of the publisher.

Manufactured in the United States of America

For
Evarts Ziegler

All magic, it goes without saying,
is illusion. The *effect* of the
illusion is how it appears to the
audience. The *preparation*
for the illusion is everything—
from the crimping of a card
to the practicing of ten thousand hours. If the preparation has been sufficient and
proper, then the execution
of the illusion is inexorable:
before you're even started,
the work is done.

By the great ones, and I would
be lying if I didn't include
myself, magic is the ultimate
entertainment: they, the audience, will never forget you,
or hold you less than kindly in
their hearts. What I'm saying, all
you beginners out there, is this:
you do it right, they can't love
you enough . . .

Merlin, Jr.

He was old, and usually he did not hunt near Melody Lake. But just before dark he had startled a decent buck, and tracked it, forgetting time. It was cold when he gave it up, and across the lake he saw the main house lit, and lower down by the shore, a single lit cabin.

The screams started coming from the cabin.

At first he thought they were female screams, but sound can be deceptive over water, and after a moment, he began to have serious doubts. They could have been coming from a man, a woman, some giant cat. Finally, he wasn't certain they came from a living throat at all.

Even with the loaded shotgun in his arms, he began to shiver. The screams drew him closer, though they had every reason not to: he was frightened, he was old, it wasn't his business, he didn't know the people, his own wife would start worrying soon.

Still the screams forced him forward.

And slowly, step by doubting step, gun ready, he moved around the water toward the sound, toward the one lit cabin and whatever was left inside . . .

1. EFFECT

1

Trust me for a while.

I understand that's *really* the line the spider hit the fly with, not "come into my parlor" as popular legend has it, and I also realize I am not always your most Walter Cronkite type fella, sturdy, staunch, etc. But in this particular instance, there is just no doubt in my you-should-pardon-the-expression mind that I know whereof I speak.

Corky thinks I'm crazy, natch.

Somebody sure is.

Doublespace.

I don't know quite how to put this without sounding unduly melodramatic, but *something*, and I wish to Christ I understood what, is happening to Corky.

He is changing.

Look—nothing wrong with change. And I'm not implying this is something out of *Invasion of the Body Snatchers* and there's some giant pod from outer space beginning to inhabit his cranium.

And I'm also aware that he's functioning full out, his career is rocketing right along and the broads he's all the time picking up never seem to have any complaints—why he always only sees them once though, I'll never figure, it's like they fall off the face of the earth or something, but his sex life isn't all that much my business, probably he bores easy—and not only is he doing good and screwing good, he's still as decent and thoughtful a guy I guess who's come down the pike of late.

But goddammit, I see signs.

Example: the moodiness. Never used to be there. And if he would get down on himself in the old days, I could always zing him a little, force some kind of rise out of him, snap him to. No more.

Now there's these long silences.

And he's closing off. He used to be so open you'd almost want to advise him to lie a little. Well he's lying now. And not just a little either.

My deepest fear? I think Corky's cracking.

Doublespace.

Query: define for those of us with less intellectual equipment than thee, oh wise one, "cracking."

A kosher Freudian would answer thusly: the state of being balmy; of having misplaced the marbles, loosened the screw.

Follow-up query: and you actually mean to conclude that just because a close friend gets quiet on occasion and on other occasions fibs—this is proof to you that he is becoming loony tunes?

No, I guess not, but I also can't sit here and ignore the fact that *this very afternoon* in front of God and everybody, he got, for the first time in his life, a migraine—can you believe that?—in the 1970's?—it's right out of a Joannie Crawford flick for chrissakes.

He was being quiet for what I thought was too long a period, so I asked, "Something the matter?"

"No, should there be?" Corky answered.

But a little too innocent for me to buy completely, so I hit him with a follow-up: "You sure been staring out the window for a while."

"I'm thinking is all."

"About?"

He shrugs. "Things."

"That's pretty specific."

"Nothing, really, just a couple little things that are maybe kind of bothering me."

"Schmucko," I said logically and soft. "If things are *bothering* you then logically, by definition, something must be the *matter*. So I simply ask again, what?"

—and he explodes—

Corky. Yelling, screaming. The same Corky who is so sweet you want to whoopse, as I never tire of pointing out to him, is insulting the shit out of me.

This is my journal, and I can put in what I want to put in and leave out what I want to leave out and I choose to leave out the details of the abuse. But it goes on and on *and on* until finally I say, "Aw Laddie, please Jesus, I was only trying to help."

He cut off then. Started to pace. Stopped. Started again. Slowed. Then the blinking. You could sense something. Now he stopped the second time. Little almost imperceptible pulsing in his temple area. He stood there and you could actually see the moment when the pain whipped down, descended like a snowfall.

Do I have to tell you I had tears behind my eyes?

Tactful comment: this is starting to seem just the least bit flitty, Fats old stick.

Honest reply: I know, I know, and we're not, but I can't help the way it sounds. "Tears." "Migraines." Sometimes I think that if me and Corky only had had one of those infinitely complicated unceasingly sado-masochistic homosexual relationships, boy, how simple life would be . . .

The Wisdom According to Fats
Entry for: 10 October, 1975

Found at: 7 Gracie Terrace
           Penthouse One
           20 October, 1975

The Contents of This
Entire Journal Will
Be Listed As:

POLICE EXHIBIT D

2

In the middle of Manhattan is the Frick, and in the middle of the Frick is the Garden Court, many columned, a gently curving glass roof over it all. There is a small fountain in the center, and the room is filled with plants imbedded in dirt so rich and black it seems almost painted. There are a few marble benches where you can sit and rest and look at the plants and listen to the quiet falling of the water. If there is a more peaceful place in the central city, it remains thus far undiscovered.

And it was in the Garden Court of the Frick Museum at close to six o'clock, on the 11th of October that Corky Withers, seated alone in the corner, began silently to weep.

The crying gave no warning, had no build. One moment he was staring at the fountain, dry-eyed, the next he was caught up in quiet tears. He reached for his handkerchief, wiped a few times, but it didn't help, so he buried his face in his hands.

"I don't suppose you want to talk."

Corky looked up into the old woman's face. He had seen her around, sometimes helping at the little stand where they sold books and postcards.

"You come here often," she said.

Corky made a nod.

"You like the paintings?"

"This room," Corky said. "It's so peaceful I feel good here."

She pointed to his face. "If this is what you're like when you feel good, I'd hate to see you when you're happy."

Corky had to laugh. After a moment, he dried his eyes. "Thank you," he said.

"Things will get better, you'll see."

"Things *are* getting better, that's what's so crazy."

She sat down alongside him on the bench. "I'm Miss Flanagan, what's your name?"

"Corky people call me."

"Why really were you crying—I'm a terrible snoop."

"You'll laugh."

"Never at tears."

"I got a piece of wonderful news yesterday."

"I'm not laughing," Miss Flanagan said. "But that's not to say I don't see the humor."

"Why are you looking at me like that?" Corky said.

"Because I've noticed you before and you've always reminded me of somebody and I just now realized who. You look like a young Spencer Tracy."

"Big ears and big nose you mean?"

She shook her head. "It's in the eyes. I believe you. You should run for president. I always thought that Spencer Tracy would have made a wonderful president."

From a doorway, a guard appeared. "Closing up shop, May."

Miss Flanagan nodded and stood. Corky did the same. "Where do you live?" he asked. "You're not the only snoop on the block."

"I have a room up in Yorkville."

"I go that way. Let me taxi you home."

"I'm not in the habit of traveling with strange men."

"I only drink blood on Tuesdays," Corky told her.

She studied his eyes. "Just like Spencer Tracy," she said, she held out her arm. "It would be my pleasure." He smiled his good smile and guided her to the street, helped her into a cab. It was the first time she had taken one, she said, in eleven years, except once when a rainstorm hit just after she'd bought a brand new pair of shoes.

They got out on the corner of 87th and First—her room was halfway in toward York—and on the corner, as he paid, she stopped and stared at the tiny jewelry shop that was closing up on the corner. She waved to the little man inside. "He's very nice, Mr. Shaber, he lets me window-shop all I want," she said when Corky came alongside.

"You do it a lot?"

"Before I go home."

"Every night?"

She nodded. "Just for a minute or two." She pointed to a lovely design of silver chains. "I always tell Mr. Shaber I'm saving for one."

Corky took her into the shop. "Gold would look better on you," he said. He pointed to a slender strand of gold. "Price, please?" he said.

"For the choker? Hundred and ten plus tax."

"Fine," Corky said and got out his wallet, put two hundred in cash on the counter, held out his hand for the choker. "Turn around," he said to Miss Flanagan.

"Don't you play games with me."

"Turn around, that's an order."

She half turned. "Why are you doing this?"

"Because I can," and he gestured for her to finish turning. When she did he put the choker around her throat, fixed the clasp properly.

She just stared at herself in the mirror, then at Corky. "Are you rich?"

He shrugged. "Not yet. Maybe I could be."

Mr. Shaber returned with the change, handed it over.

Miss Flanagan was looking at herself in the mirror again. "It's really mine?"

"Oh stop it."

"You don't think it's too tight or anything?"

"I think it's just the newness of the feel," Mr. Shaber told her. "Wear it awhile. I can always have it made a little longer if you decide."

"'Night," Corky said, and he opened the door for her.

As they turned onto 87th she said, "Thank you but I really want to know why you're doing this."

"I don't know. You made me laugh when I was crying. I like to please people."

"Have you done this kind of thing before?"

"Never. Probably never will again."

"What can I do in exchange?"

"You don't get it, May—we're even now."

"Can I at least make you some coffee?"

"I'm not in the habit of coffee-ing with strange women."

She laughed, touched the gold. "It does feel tight."

"Probably just the newness."

"Will you have coffee?"

"I'll walk you to your door. Maybe you'll change your mind, not want me inside."

"No. I trust you."

"Everybody does."

"Is there any reason they shouldn't?"

Corky felt his eyes go cold. "Not for me to say . . ."

3

THE MYSTERY OF THE GOLDEN CHOKER

I'm not about to knock Georges or Dame Agatha off their thrones, but right from the start, as soon as I saw the thing, I knew it was weirdo time. I asked, as casually as only I can, what the fuck it was.

Corky shrugged, as casually as only he can. "Just a thing. Choker I think they're called."

"And we're wearing gold this year, is that it, Hermione?"

"It's not mine."

"Possession is nine-tenths, schmucko."

He looked at me. "Please. I would really appreciate it more than you can imagine if we don't pursue this."

"I'm not pursuing, who's pursuing, but when somebody spends what must be a grand for a hunk of jewelry, can you blame me since I'm only known far and wide as being that somebody's manager, for being a little interested?"

"It didn't even cost hardly a hundred." Corky got out a cigarette. "Want one?"

I said sure and we smoked awhile.

"Don't do this, huh? I asked please," he said finally.

"Just smoking is all I'm doing," I told him.

"It's the silence."

"You want I should put on my tap shoes and do my Annette Funicello routine?"

"It was just an impulse. I bought it for Miss Flanagan, she's an old lady."

"Oh I believe that. I get those impulses hourly. I'm acquiring the Taj Mahal for the milkman tomorrow."

He's starting to pace now, inhaling tense and deep. "It was too tight for her. She asked me to take it back. The jeweler said he'd loosen it but when I got to the store he was shut so I'll take it in later."

"Why the impulse?"

He looked at me. "You'll make more out of it than I feel like just now."

"Why the impulse?"

"You just gonna keep on saying that?"

"Throughout eternity, Heathcliff—why the impulse?"

He wouldn't look at me and he was talking licketyfuckingsplit. "I was at the Frick, I was listening to the fountain, I started to cry, Miss Flanagan works there, she got me out of my mood, I felt I owed her something, no big deal, see?"

"You *cried?* In *public?*"

"I knew you'd make more—"

"—just hold it—day before yesterday, you play Babs Stanwyck and get a migraine—which just happened to be the day the agency called and said there was some tv interest. The next day, weeping, which just happened to be the day the agency called again to say things were starting to simmer on the tv deal."

Corky put out his cigarette.

"Why couldn't this legendary Miss Flanagan take the choker back to the jeweler herself?"

"I volunteered."

"I don't believe you. I think you're hiding something."

"What would I be hiding?"

"I don't know—call the Frick and get her on the phone—"

"—no reason—"

"—all right, *I'll* call her. Flanagan you say?" I start to dial information for the Frick.

He's got his hand on mine, stopping the dialing. "She won't be there, I just remembered."

I waited.

"She was going on vacation. That's right. She won't be back for a while. She told me that. While we were having coffee. I just remembered now."

I still waited, staring at him.

"I want you to say you believe me."

"Oh Laddie, 'course I do," and I hit the sincerity with all I had and he bought it. Then I did a quick subject change. Creasey or Erle Stanley would have probably kept hacking away, but who can deal with those kinda consequences, not me. I mean, what if it was all a lie? Or worse, what if it was all true, and he's losing control bad, tears for the world to see. Or worse, what if it's kind of true. And there is a Miss Flanagan. Or was, maybe, till yesterday . . .

Doublespace.

The Wisdom According to Fats
Entry for: 12 October, 1975

Found at: 7 Gracie Terrace
            Penthouse One
            20 October, 1975

The Contents of This
Entire Journal Will
Be Listed As:

POLICE EXHIBIT D

4

"In that book, y'know, you kill me."

Corky looked at the fat girl, smiled. He took her arm when the light changed, guided her across 66th Street.

"Did you read it?"

"*Looking for Mr. Goodbar?*" Corky shook his head. It was almost midnight and they hadn't even gotten to her place yet.

"But you know about it?"

"Sort of by default; any girl in a singles place brings it up sooner or later. I guess by mentioning it they figure they'll ward off evil spirits."

"Are you an evil spirit?"

"I wish I was that colorful," Corky said.

She didn't smile or anything.

Corky stopped on the sidewalk. "Hey, you're very frightened."

"Um-hmm." Then: "Should I be?"

"I'm very gentle," Corky said, very gently. Then: "All my victims say that."

She still would not smile.

"Now you please listen, okay? It's late, and you've probably got to get up early for work tomorrow, and there's no *law* says we've got to do anything at all, either with or to each other. Let me walk you to your door and we'll call it quits. Or I can leave you here if you'd like."

"Are you always so considerate or is it an act?"

"I don't know. It's an act." He thought about that. "No, it isn't."

She started walking. "Come on," she said. "I trust you. Why do you think that is?"

Corky shrugged. "People do."

"Always?"

"Pretty much."

"To their regret?"

"You're still frightened."

"I'm down to edgy."

"Have you ever been picked up before?"

"That's what's so crazy, this is my forty-sixth time."

Corky broke out laughing.

"Why is that funny?"

"I don't know; the accuracy surprised me."

She gestured to the canopy just ahead. "I'm in there."

Corky escorted her to the door. There was an old man asleep inside, clad in what was once a uniform. "Up to you," he said.

She studied his face. "You don't even remember my name, do you?"

"You *said* your name was Diana, but you probably lied."

She sort of smiled, did nod. "On the money. Really I'm Fern." Now she looked at him. "I'll bet you're not really Charles, though, are you?"

"It takes a lot out of you when you lie, so I try to avoid it whenever possible. Charles Withers, that's me. Most everybody calls me Corky."

"I can't make you out."

"You're not supposed to, Diana slash Fern. My God, I've spent a whole lifetime getting my disguise on straight, you think I want just anybody seeing through it without at least a little effort?"

"I'm not just anybody."

"I can tell that, Fern my beloved; it's really quite apparent, Diana my sweet—you take longer making up your mind than just anybody. But we are now in the crunch. Do we go up or do we part? Because we have prattled enough in this October night and frankly, although I don't know you well enough to be poetic, my ass is freezing standing here."

She gestured inside. "Oh, we go up. We always go up. Almost always anyway. I just like dragging things out if I can."

"Well feel proud, you've done royally."

"Corky? You were never an 'almost.'"

"Gratefully received," Corky said.

"You talk nice and I like your face," Fern said. She glanced up at him. "Besides," and for a moment, she paused.

Corky waited.

"You look familiar . . ."

"You're still dragging things out," Corky called from the bed.

Inside the bathroom, the sink went off, the door half opened. "What?" Fern from behind the door.

"You are awaited," Corky told her.

"Give me one sec more; I've got a cleanliness thing, you don't mind?"

"Just so you wear the spike heels and the rubber suit, I'll forgive anything."

She laughed, closed the door. Again, water from the sink.

Corky lay on his side, studying the door, wondering if he should have picked up the one with the body instead. Fern had a pretty face in spite of her flesh, but the other one, the one two stools down, had been splendidly stacked. Corky had wavered, wondering which he should try for, and from the way the built one had watched him, he felt there was a decent chance she would prove accommodating. But something about the aggression in her, some shoulder set perhaps or maybe just the way she gripped her glass, made him decide no. The one with the body looked like a libber—"you can screw me, buddy, but lemme tell you, you're gonna *suffer*"—and he was in no mood for grappling.

The sound of the sink continued. Nothing to do but wait. Corky waited, eyes now closed.

> . . . Peggy Ann Snow
> Peggy Ann Snow
> Please let me follow
> Wherever you go . . .

Corky blinked. The little poem always had a way of surprising him, arriving almost unbidden from somewhere inside. No matter what girl he slept with or how many, at some point Peg would appear, just to let him know she was still around.

"Duh-dumm." Fern stood in the doorway, pretty face shining, a large towel held in front of her large body.

"Worth the wait," Corky said.

She nodded toward the bed lamp on his side. "I'm the shy type."

"You haven't got a corner on the market, I'm still wearing my underwear." He flicked the room into darkness. She crossed to the bed with the speed of familiarity and then she was beside him. He reached for her, pulled her close.

She touched him. "You aren't either wearing anything," Fern said, surprised, for a moment, childlike.

"Trying to make you happy."

"Make me happy."

Corky was gentle with women. He had started late, and when he first began socializing, that gentleness was probably born of plain blind panic, but it seemed to work well, and it came naturally to him, so he never felt the need to change. Now, slowly, he began touching Fern's body, the tips of his fingers tracing mindless patterns on her skin.

"Fern," he whispered.

"What?"

"Try and remember one thing."

"Tell me."

"This isn't a dentist's appointment."

"Am I that tense?"

"I would say so."

"It takes me a while to get in the swing of things."

"I'll be right here waiting."

"Listen?"

"Sure."

"I'm sorry, usually I relax faster."

"Time is not one of our major problems," Corky said, gentle and soft, and then he kissed her, kissed her again, ran the tip of his tongue along her neck. She reached for him, held him

too tight, feigned passion. He waited for her to unclasp and
when she did he began the soft touching again, his fingertips
moving constantly now, circling her breasts, moving around
without quite approaching, and she held him again, this time
the passion less feigned, and they kissed, she relaxed a bit
more, and now his fingers grazed her soft breasts, touching
the flesh, not the nipple, keeping a fine rhythm going until her
nipple began to distend and harden and

> . . . Peggy Ann Snow
> Peggy Ann Snow
> Please let me follow—

"Corky?"

"Shh."

"No. Really. Listen, I hate people who ask 'what are you
thinking' but what are you thinking?"

"It doesn't matter."

"I did something wrong, didn't I?—that's why you hesitated?—what did I do?"

"A girl I had a crush on, that's all."

"When?"

"I haven't seen her in fifteen years."

"So why'd you think of her now?"

'For sustenance' he couldn't say. 'Because I always do'
wasn't much better. "I guess you must remind me of her,"
Corky said.

"I like that," Fern said.

Corky kissed her breasts.

"That too," from Fern, softer this time.

The pace picked up then. She was relaxing easily and he
felt in control. Besides, there was something occasionally
pleasant about being with an overweight woman—especially
when they were still young enough to have flesh tone. No
matter where Corky placed his skilled hands, there was nothing to jar him, nothing sharp to injure. It was a round world
he was visiting, and getting there was probably a quarter of
the fun. Their bodies were in synch now, and when she was

moist he was ready, so he moved in, being careful to keep his weight off her as he rolled on top, because she was, if the signals she was sending were to be believed, enjoying herself thoroughly and he had no wish to add any discomfort; balanced on his elbows and knees, Corky moved in happy silence, a silence that went on for he hadn't really any exact idea, but it ended when Fern said *"The Carson show!"* quite loudly.

"Yes?"

"No wonder you looked familiar—my God, I saw you on *The Johnny Carson Show*, you were a guest after Don Rickles, that's right, isn't it?"

Corky stopped what he was doing. "Right."

"I'm fucking somebody famous, that's just so wonderful."

"I'm not famous."

"Oh but you will be, I know it—you were sensational, better than Rickles—I swear to God I'm not just saying that because you're here."

Corky said nothing. Could-not-say-anything.

"Just wait till I tell them at Brearley—I teach at Brearley, that's a school . . ." Her voice lost the excitement. "No one would believe me. 'Famous Man Fucks Fat Girl.' I wouldn't believe it either." She was quiet a moment. "To hell with 'em, I won't tell anyone." She moved out, groped around for the bed lamp, turned it on. "But I'll know, won't I?"

Corky made a nod.

She reached up, touched his face. "You know what, Mr. Withers? You are my memory now . . ."

Corky waited till she turned the light off. Then he put his lips to her throat. Her throat was lovely . . .

5

Fats was sprawled in an armchair, the latest *Variety* nearby.
Corky came out of the bedroom. He had been lying down in
his slacks and button-down, and now the pants were wrinkled,
the shirt torn. Nobody said anything for a moment. Corky
walked slowly to the window and opened the blinds. The October sun wasn't all that strong, but even so, it made him cry
out with sudden pain. Quickly he closed the blinds again,
yanked them tight shut.

"Schmucko," Fats said then. "You and me have got to have
a powwow."

"No we don't," Corky told him. He glanced at his watch.
"Christ, how long was I in there?"

"I don't know; two hours, more maybe, what difference
does it make?"

"Curious is all."

"What you mean is, are they getting worse?"

"You blame me for wondering?"

"You're the only one that can answer that." Long pause.
"Are they?"

Another. Longer. Then: "I think."

"That's two migraines right?—the *first* migraines of your
life, let's not forget, and you stand there and say we don't
have to talk?"

"Nothing to talk about. I'm fine now."

"Sure you are: your hands are twitching, your eyes are all
sunk in, your face is the color of cream-of-fucking-wheat—we
all look like that when we're fine."

Corky turned away. "Go easy on the sarcasm, huh?"

"Aw Christ, Laddie, I'm *worried*, that's all."

"I know."

"Butt me?"

Corky got out cigarettes for each of them, lit them both.

"Anything happen last night?" Fats asked.

"You mean anything so unusual it would cause a goddam migraine? Don't you think that's reaching?"

"*Spiel.*"

"I picked up a girl, bought her a couple drinks, went home with her."

"And?"

"You want me to get graphic? You want a rundown on the texture of her thighs?"

"Let me be the smart ass, okay? Now you're with this girl and it went fine?"

"It did for me. I think she was kind of sorry to see me go. She even asked would I sign her Latin textbook."

"*Textbook*—was this a school kid you were boffing?"

"No, no, a teacher, at Brearley; very fancy place."

"Sounds it—at least one of their teachers is a hooker with a signature fetish—that's just the kind of fine outstanding individual I want getting my kids ready to face life."

"It's perfectly logical—she caught the *Carson* show and liked it and anyway, you don't have any kids."

"If I did, I wouldn't send them to this Brearley—my God, I wonder what the gym teacher's into?"

Corky started laughing.

"It wasn't that funny," Fats said.

"I thought it was."

"No. I'm onto something and you're trying to throw me off the track—did she know who you were right off?"

Corky hesitated.

"Before or after—when did she recognize you?"

"During."

"Oh Laddie. That's got to be it."

"You telling me that's significant, Doctor?"

"You telling me it isn't . . . ? What happened after she recognized you?"

"She just turned on the lights and looked at me."

"And after that?"

"When it was dark again you mean? I guess I kissed her throat."

"And then?"

Corky shook his head. "That would be telling . . ."

6

The Postman was kind of a legend. For many reasons, most notably two. (1) He was the only agent *now* operating who had been given his nickname by Jolson. This was back in the 20's, a summer Sunday and the singer needed a large amount of cash; hard to find now, harder then. But Ben Greene—the Postman's given appellation—had scrounged up the proper amount, handed it to the pleased performer at a large luncheon party. Jolson had put his arm around the then kid, and said out loud, "This one is gonna be heard from—he's like the Postman, he always comes through." For the ensuing half century, the Postman he had been.

(2) He was the only agent *ever* operating who had moved through all the branches of show business with never a remotely bad year carrying all that while the single stigmata that had ruined so many careers: he wasn't Jewish. "How is such a thing possible?" he would thunder. "How such a miracle? Was it because I was more brilliant? Yes, but that wasn't all. Because I was more industrious? Yes, but others labored and fell by the wayside. The secret was simply this:"—and here he would pause, drop his voice to as close as it would come to a whisper—"I triumphed because, with a name like Ben Greene, how could I possibly be gentile?" Then he would wait for his laugh, timing it perfectly, always.

Probably he should have been an actor—he was, in fact, a compulsive and not unskilled amateur magician—and he cultivated his theatricality whenever possible. "You are looking at a fella who is criminally flamboyant," he liked to say. "Christ, I *invented* conspicuous consumption." It might have been true —he was terribly rich. "For many reasons," he liked to say;

"most notably three: I had big earning years when there weren't a lot of taxes, but that's not as important as investing sensibly, which I also did, but that's not as important as marrying an heiress, which I also did." And then a pause. "God bless and rest her soul."

He became, on his wife's death, the chief stockholder in one of the three largest hairbrush companies in the world, which only proved, he liked to say, that God had a sense of humor, since the Postman had been bald before even Jolson came into his life. Frail and small, bald and weak-eyed, with the energy of the truly driven. "If they could harness me, Con Ed could light the world."

He was long past retirement age, but the Morris people let him keep his office and work when he wanted. "They're kind to me," he liked to say. "For many reasons, most notably one: if they're not, they know goddam well I'll buy the company and fire the fuckers."

He adored money. He knew, to the half dollar, how he had done that day on the market. Whenever possible he liked getting hourly reports and was constantly computing on table-cloths, coming out with statements like "I lost eleven thousand dollars during coffee." Gain or loss, it never bothered him.

Because the purpose of money was to spend. "I am unabashedly *oldveau riche*," he liked to say; "nobody my age is allowed to be *nouveau* anything." Only the best would satisfy, and if he couldn't get the best, he got the most expensive. Which was why he drove a white Corniche convertible, and smoked only Monte Cruz Individuales, and drank only Lafite until he found that Petrus was selling for higher, so he switched brand allegiance overnight. And why, since it had made its comeback, he lunched, daily, at least this year, at the corner table farthest from the door of The Four Seasons . . .

Corky hated fancy places. Overstatement. He had not been to enough of them to develop anything approximating hatred. But he disliked them plenty. It was mainly a matter of belonging—all the other people in whatever rich room he found himself—their credentials were in order, they understood the dimensions, got the decorum right. Corky simply felt false—he had no business being there, soon he'd be found out, then thrown out, humiliated publicly, never the happiest way.

When the Postman had invited him to lunch, Corky tried to make it an office meeting but the old man wouldn't hear of it, simply said, "The Seasons, tomorrow, one, g'bye," and rang off.

Now, Corky stalked the sidewalk across from the restaurant. He had waited until he had seen the Postman go in—if he had arrived first, they never would have seated him, they would have spotted right off he didn't belong in a nice place like that, they would have blown him right back to the street with their laughter.

But if the Postman was already there, he would be all right, could just walk right up to the reservations man and say, "Mr. Ben Greene is expecting me, I'm positive he is," and they would nod and ask for him to follow and then once he got to the Postman's table, no one would ever dare to throw him out, he was safe.

He opened the door to the restaurant, walked past the coat checking room, up the stairs to the reservations desk. Halfway up the stairs more accurately.

That was when the reservations man glanced at Corky's throat—where he didn't have a necktie.

Corky froze.

The reservations man went back to his lists.

Why do you do this to yourself? You should have worn a tie or called and asked if one was necessary. Either way. But you do not go to a place like this place improperly attired.

Unless you *want* to get thrown out.

Corky began to fidget. The reservations man looked up again, again at the bare throat.

I don't want to get thrown out. I don't court failure. True.

"Were you looking for someone, sir?" the reservations man said from behind his small desk.

Corky nodded.

The reservations man gestured for him to come nearer.

Corky did.

"Who did you wish to see?"

I'm sorry about the necktie, Corky was about to say. It was just a mistake, I didn't mean anything, Corky almost said. Instead he said, "Ben Greene," and the reservations man said, "Of course, follow me," and smiled—*smiled*—

See? You're as good as any of 'em.

He walked across the room, passing all the wealthy people who belonged there.

As any of 'em!

The Postman was waiting in the corner. "Have I got news for you. Sit. Want a drink?"

"I figured you did when you called. No, nothing."

"Have a cigar," the Postman said, handing over an Individuale. "Four bucks each. I got a special deal, Dunhill's loves me, I get 'em ten for forty."

Corky put it into his inside blazer pocket. "For later. Thank you. What's the good news?"

"I'm building the suspense, don't interrupt." He handed over another Individuale. "Take two, they're big."

Corky nodded, slid the second cigar beside the first.

"How's your manager?" the Postman asked, with his usual sour smile; Fats always referred to him, both in public and anywhere else, as "Gangrene," which the Postman felt a bit undignified for one of his years.

"Fats is imfuckingpossible as always," Corky said, imitating Fats flawlessly.

"What's that speck on your blazer?" the Postman asked, reaching across the table and Corky tried not to smile because there wasn't much he could do about it, it was magic time.

The Postman's hand burst into flame.

Corky did his best to look surprised.

"Pretty good, wouldn't you say?" the Postman said. "Brand-new flash paper—improved—Tannen's just got in a shipment." Tannen's was the best magic store probably anywhere, with a catalog hundreds of pages long. The Postman owned at least one of almost every trick they sold and spent as many hours per week as he could talking with the magicians who used the place as a clubhouse when they were in town.

"You really fooled me," Corky said.

"You shouldda worn a necktie," the Postman said, going into his right-hand suit pocket. "Here." And he pulled out a blue silk scarf. "This'll go nice with your blazer," and he handed it out to Corky, but by the time Corky had gotten it, the Postman had run it through his hands and the scarf was now green. The Postman winked at Corky. "Pretty good, wouldn't you say?"

"Yessir." Then: "Do you think we could get to the good news now?"

"Show is over." The Postman nodded, and he reached into his inside pocket. "No more magic, you got my word. Here's the terms I've worked out—" He stopped suddenly, looking at his hand. "Why, what's this I found? Look, Corky, it's a sponge ball, I wonder how it got there? Looks like an ordinary sponge ball to me, what do you think?" He held it out for Corky to examine.

"Very ordinary," Corky said.

"Let's just see," the Postman went on, a certain practiced note coming into his voice now. "I have a strange feeling this just might be one of those rare sponge balls recently discovered off the coast of Tibet—surely you've read about the mysterious disappearing Tibetan miracle balls."

"I haven't; nossir."

"They disappear, Corky. If you squeeze them hard enough, they turn into atmosphere. Now I'm probably a little too old, my fingers probably lack the strength, but let's just see."

Corky watched as the Postman put the ball between his hands and exerted pressure.

"Amazing," Corky said.

"Hold on, goddammit," the Postman said, "it ain't gone yet," and he opened his hands, showing the tiny sponge ball. He started to squeeze again, making little grunt sounds as he did. "*Now* you can say 'amazing,'" the Postman said, opening his hands, the ball gone. He winked at Corky. "Pretty good, wouldn't you say?"

Corky nodded.

The Postman pulled off his thumb tip with the sponge ball inside, stuffed it into his pocket. Then he just looked at Corky for a long time, studying him.

"What's wrong?" Corky said finally.

"I'm trying to freeze you like you are right now—you'd be doing the both of us a favor if you'd do it too. Remember who we are that's sitting here."

Corky waited.

"You're a good kid, Cork. I've been a little bit around—I was Cain's agent when he went in the ring against Abel—and I've seen it a thousand times out of a thousand: you hit it big, you turn shitheel. That's an automatic. I'd love it if you'd beat the odds."

"Maybe I won't hit it big," Corky said.

"Two years ago, you couldn't get arrested; two years from now you're gonna have it all. I conned CBS into giving you the pilot special. Which, as you might have guessed, is the reason I've called us all together."

Very quickly Corky said, "What's a pilot special?"

"How old are you?"

"Just over thirty."

"How can you be so old and so stupid?—My Christ, when I was your age I'd already turned down Jean Harlow as a client."

Corky put his hands in his lap, made sure they'd stay there.

"A pilot special," the Postman went on, "is like what they gave Rich Little last year. When they're hot for somebody—and believe me, I didn't con anybody at CBS, Goldstone wants you—they do a special that if it delivers, off you go. Bob Hope does a special, it's part of a bigger contract. So many shows, so many years. With you, they're kind of testing."

"And it's all set and everything?"

"It's set, but it's not set-set, if you follow me. There's boiler plate to be slugged out, and they want to know what kind of publicity will *you* do free and we got to find out what kind of publicity will *they* do free, and we got the medical exam to go through, and I'm willing to gamble on taking less for you if they'll go a little higher on the total budget for the show, and on and on, agent bullshit. But the bottom line is, we want it we got it, what do you have to say? You want to kiss my hand, I don't mind."

Silence.

"May I quote you on that?" the Postman wondered.

Corky began to shake his head.

"What's that supposed to mean?"

"I don't think I want to take the medical exam," Corky said.

The Postman shrugged. "Okay, I'll try and see about getting it waived. Any special reason?"

"Just principle."

"I don't get it."

"Okay. I don't know if I can explain this but don't get impatient. For openers, how long have we known each other?"

"What, two years, little more? You were working that place in Los Angeles—"

"—the Stardust."

The Postman nodded.

"You'll never know how important that night was for me. You came ambling back, in that shy way you have, kind of indicating 'don't look now, folks, but God just walked in—'"

"I don't do that," the Postman said. "Do I do that?" He shrugged. "'Course, it's not totally untrue, go on."

"You came backstage and said who you were and did I know and I said of course I knew and you said you were about to give me the break of my life and sign me up as a client." Corky looked at the old man a minute. "Do you remember what I answered?"

"Effing well I remember—you said I could *represent* you but you wouldn't *sign*. I had to karate chop the agency into going along with that."

"That was principle," Corky said. "I knew what you could mean to me but I never would have signed—because if you're happy with me and I'm happy with you, *we don't need to sign.* Our *word* is all we have and that's plenty. For me anyway."

"But what's with the medical exam? Why is that principle?"

"They're saying there's something *wrong* with me, don't you see that? I say I'm fine, and they say, we don't trust you, we want our doctors to go around looking inside. *We'll* tell you if you're fine."

"There isn't anything wrong with you?"

"'Course not."

The Postman looked at Corky for a while. "Are you serious about this principle thing?"

"Serious?"

"That's right. Is it a dealbreaker?"

Corky shrugged. "I guess it is."

The Postman raised his eyes to anyone up there. "Performers," he said. "I should have been a cesspool cleaner like my mother wanted," he said. Then he took a silver dollar out of his pocket and turned it into gold . . .

7

WHAT IS THIS PRINCIPLES BULLSHIT?

Doublespace.

Not that I'm upset but WHERE ALL OF A SUDDEN DO THESE FUCKING PRINCIPLES COME FROM?

Calm down.

Not so easy. When you consider that all we have busted our humps for is just a prayer for a shot at making it big. Why has all that sweat been spilled? I try going over and over the ecofuckingnomics of it with him.

He won't listen.

"Corky," I say to him. "Let's not waste our time contemplating the twenty-five thousand we'd get for doing the special. That's just walking around money. Just contemplate what happens if the pilot special gets picked up. Gangrene could gouge us an easy fifty thou per show. *Fifty thousand.* Suppose we only do one season. Twenty shows. That's a million, schmucko. Six zeros following the one."

"This is just the kind of thing you'll never understand."

I go into my big pitch.

"What if we don't bomb?" I begin. "Suppose we turn into Andy Williams or Ann-Margret. Give us a five-year run, let's be conservative. Five million.—And Vegas?—I mean, a tv headliner only gets maybe a hundred and fifty *per week.*—Forever.—My God, Dean Martin was pulling his drunk act on the plebes out there since before Carlo Gambino had a police record and he's still hot.—They're faithful in Vegas.—They're foul weather friends.—So," I sum up to old buddy Cork; "so what we've got is enough to pay the bills a year or so no matter what, and if we charm the people enough, all we've got is a minimum six figures for life."

"Sorry, it's a matter of principle, I won't take the medical exam."

He won't let some ancient hacksaw see if he's still got a knee jerk.

"WHY?WHY?WHY?

"Please God," I beg, "tell me."

"Principles."

"You're not letting me in on something, admit it."

"Don't bug me, principles are principles."

"Principles," I scream, "are guys you got sent to see for smoking in the boys' room."

He laughs. "I wish I could be funny like you."

"Is it the migraines?"

"For the millionth time—"

"—brain cancer?—you think they're gonna find something just terrible inside?"

Silence.

"Is that it, Laddie?"

Silence.

"If there is something wrong, let's for God's sake find it now, while we can do something."

"THERE'S NOTHING TO FIND, FATS, NOW LET ME ALONE."

"THIS SHOW IS OUR FUTURE AND I WANT IT."

Double silence.

Loooooooooooooooooooooonnnnnnng one.

Then: Him: "Listen, I'm sure the Postman will get them to waive the medical."

"Yeah? And if he doesn't?"

He didn't have the answer and neither do I. All I know is that *if* he doesn't, there's gonna be blood.

And not mine.

The Wisdom According to Fats
Entry for: 17 October, 1975

Found at: 7 Gracie Terrace
Penthouse One
20 October, 1975

The Contents of This
Entire Journal Will
Be Listed As:

POLICE EXHIBIT D

8

"I couldn't budge 'em," came the Postman's voice.

Corky held tight to the phone.

"You still there, kid?"

"I thought you said Goldstone wanted me—"

"—he does but—"

"—did you explain about the principle?—"

"—this is company policy—"

"—it was company policy when I wouldn't sign with you—"

"—this is *legal*—they're not about to spend half a million on a special and then find out on taping day there's a health problem—"

"—there's no problem—"

"—Corky—"

"—*you make them understand!—*" Corky said, and he slammed down the phone. He started walking crazily around the desk. "You heard all that?"

"I'm not saying doodledyfucking doo," Fats told him. "You dug this hole."

"You're with the Postman."

"I know you gotta take that exam."

"*Well I won't.*"

"*Then tell me what this is all about!*"

Corky went to his left temple, started to rub.

"Don't pull one of those migraines now goddammit—"

The phone rang again.

"Hello?—"

"Listen, I'm coming over—"

Harder at the temple. "No reason."

"We got to talk."

"About what?"

"Kid, are you afraid to take it?"

"No."

"And you're telling me everything?"

"I don't know, what's everything?"

"I'm coming right now—"

"—I won't be here—"

"—Kid—listen to the Postman—"

"—I mean it—you come and I'm gone—"

"—I'll take the goddam thing with you—how's that for an offer—Christ, I've had cancer, I got emphysema, my varicose veins are in all the best medical texts—if I'm not afraid to take it, what have you got to worry about?"

"I'm—not—afraid."

"Just wait right there."

Corky heard the click. He put the phone down. "I'm going."

"Where?"

"I'm not sure—you coming or not?"

"You want me?"

"*I'm not sure—you coming or not?*"

"Tell me where you're going."

Quietly then: ". . . home?"

"You haven't got a home."

Quieter still: ". . . tell me something I don't know . . ."

2. PREPARATION

MUTT

First picture: Joe and his girl standing on the beach. Bully with Muscles shouts across the sand—"Hey SKINNY! . . . yer ribs are showing!"

Corky Withers, nearing 10, examined the Charles Atlas ad over and over. No point to it, all wasted effort; he knew the thing by heart. Still, better safe than sorry.

Second picture: Joe and his girl still on the beach. Bully with Muscles standing with them now. Joe's girl (worried): "Don't let him hit you, Joe." Joe (to Bully with Muscles): "Watch what you say, fella . . ." Bully with Muscles (shoving Joe in the face): "Shut up, you bag of bones!"

Corky lay on his back and studied the ceiling. What a terrible thing that must have been for Joe. Nothing you could do but stand there and take it. Sure, you could try and hit the big guy, but that's what he wanted, the chance to make mincemeat out of you, leave you bloody on the sand, steal your girl, maybe kiss her if it got dark.

Corky got up and walked to the mirror. He took off his shirt and looked at his chest. There was no doubt about it: he was skinny and his ribs were showing. He made his arm stiffen and flexed it, forming as big a muscle as he could. Holding his right arm that way, he moved next to the mirror and examined the result: it didn't seem possible but his bicep looked *smaller* flexed than normal. Corky skipped back to the bed and grabbed for his comic book.

Third picture: Joe, alone and miserable in his room, talking to himself. Joe: "Darn it! I'm tired of being a skinny scarecrow. Charles Atlas says he can make me a new man! I'll gamble a stamp and get his FREE BOOK."

Corky went over the ad very carefully, because here was the tricky part: between the third picture and the fourth there was one large diagonal word:

How much later though, that was the thing they didn't tell you exactly. Fourth picture: Joe, still alone, still talking to himself, watching himself in the mirror, only now he had *muscles*. Joe: "Boy! It didn't take long. What a build. Now I'll take care of that bully."

God, Corky thought, if I could do that overnight, would I knock them on their keisters tomorrow at breakfast. Mutt would be sitting in the kitchen, blowing on his steaming coffee and big brother Willie would be spooning in the Wheaties and here I'd come, only I wouldn't make any big deal about it, I'd just walk in casually in my bathing trunks and maybe flex a couple times and ask for the milk and Mutt would say, "Corky, my God" and I'd say, "Something wrong, Dad?" and he'd say, "Corky, my God, what happened to you overnight?" and I'd kind of expand my chest until Mutt's eyes practically popped and he'd say, "Corky, I never seen a build like that, you look even stronger than Willie and he's eight years older than you" and then Willie the football star would say, "Wanna trader six inchers?" and I'd kind of yawn and nod and then he'd cream me on the arm, only cheating, drawing his hand back at least ten inches, slamming all he had and he'd wring his hand and cry "Oww, Jesus, Dad, the kid's a rock" and I'd say, "When are you going to hit me?" and he'd say, "I did already, Jesus Dad, he's so powerful he didn't even feel it and I hit him hard enough to drop most guys" and I'd say, "Here's a love-tap from your bag of bones brother" and zap him a little and Willie the football star would go "Jesus Dad I think he broke my arm . . ."

Overnight was probably unrealistic, Corky decided, studying the fourth picture carefully. Even though Atlas built muscles fast, you couldn't go from being skinny to a superpower in one day, no matter how hard you tried. At the very least, it had to take a week.

Fifth picture: Joe and his girl back on the beach. The girl is watching as Joe smashes the Bully with Muscles so hard on the chin there were stars around the Bully with Muscles' face. And all Joe said was, casually: "Here's a love-tap—from that 'Bag of Bones.' Remember?"

Last picture: Joe standing there, nothing but raw power. His girl clinging to one arm. Joe's girl (love in her eyes?): "Oh Joe! You *are* a real he-man, after all." And in the background, two beautiful girls saying at the same time to each other: "And he used to be so skinny!"

And above them all, in big big letters surrounded by a sunburst:

WHAT

A

MAN

Corky stuck his feet up on his wall and lay that way awhile, right-angled.

WHAT

A

MAN

What must the world be like when people actually said that kind of thing about you? "What a man that Corky Withers is." You walk along and people just come up to you and say, "Oh Corky, you *are* a real he-man after all." And wherever he went on the streets of Normandy would be this trailing whisper: ". . . and he used to be so skinny . . ."

Everyone would know inside a day. Normandy just wasn't big enough for secrets. It was your standard Catskill town, ninety miles from New York, nine from Grossinger's, ringed with mountains, and totally dependent on outsiders for survival.

Naturally, everyone would be looking for you to get conceited, so you couldn't let that happen. And you couldn't let your grades slip either, although that wasn't likely in his case.

As good as big brother Willie was in sports, he was at whittling. And as good as he was at whittling, he was twice that good in school. It used to bother him sometimes that it wasn't harder. For a while, through third grade at least, he had tried to make it seem harder, tried to act nervous when it was quiz time, used to worry aloud at recess that he'd goofed. But after a while he stopped the feigning, it wasn't working anyway. He wasn't necessarily smart, he decided, but he was good at school. Even before he was ten, he knew there was a difference, which probably meant that he was both smart *and* good at school, but he never much bothered pursuing the thought.

Besides, Mutt didn't give a damn.

Maybe if his mother had stayed around, she would have done sufficient oohing and stuff, but she'd had it one winter evening, when Corky was eight, just packed and fled for Oregon with an equally unhappy plumber from the other side of town.

Corky was the only one she told beforehand. She came into his room late one night going "shhhh" and smelling, as she always did, of sherry wine. She crossed the dark room, sat on the edge of his bed, and got right to it. "I'm gonna miss you, Cork," she said.

Corky waited in the night.

"You gotta promise not to think bad, but when you get a shot at waking up without a hangover 'cause you don't need the booze, you gotta take it, you'll understand that someday."

Corky nodded.

"Ferd's waiting outside in the pickup, I can't take but a sec', I just hadda give you a wet one for good-bye."

She kissed him then.

"Drunk as a skunk," she said. "Wow, I bent down too fast, the whole place is spinning."

"Don't go," Corky said. "I promise I'll be good."

"You *are* good, Cork. You don't cry, you do nice things, you clean up your room without no one telling you. You want the truth why I came back tonight?"

Corky nodded.

"To pick up the menagerie you made for me." He had given her a half dozen tiny animals he'd whittled for Christmas. "That and the heart." The wooden heart he'd made for her birthday. She touched her purse. "Got 'em all in here." She stood. "Gonna miss me?"

". . . oh Jeez—"

"—come on now."

Corky got control.

"That's my Cork."

"Will you write? I'll whittle you a merry-go-round for Christmas if you'll write. It'll turn and everything."

"If I can, you know I will."

Corky knew a 'no' when he heard one.

"Bye, Cork."

"What about them?"

"Willie don't care about nothing but sports and Mutt only cares about Willie. If you play your cards right and don't tell him, I don't think Mutt'll know I'm gone."

The truth of it was she was probably right; at least Mutt never mentioned her name again. At least not when Corky was around.

Mutt was small and he was tough and the Gods had pissed on him all his life—his way of putting it—and for proof he always showed his legs—the right was a good inch and a half shorter than the other. He'd been born that way and if he hadn't, there wouldn't have been a stadium big enough to hold his fans. He knew that in his feisty heart. Grange would have been trash and the Four Horsemen would have been dogmeat alongside him. Maybe Bronko Nagurski might have been his equal, but no one else, *no one.*

Except he couldn't run well, not well enough, not with his legs, and if the Gods pissed on you, there wasn't a shelter anywhere you could hide, so he never heard the cheers, never saw the girls dance and wave, he gave rubdowns at Grossinger's and talked sports with the guests.

And made Willie Withers a star. He fed him right, nursed him through muscle pulls, taught him moves, drove him, drove him, and when Willie was a freshman he ran back a punt for a touchdown the first time he touched the ball and by the end of that season he was Willie the Wisp Withers, the biggest thing in Normandy since ever . . .

Corky got off his bed and went into his big brother's room. Willie was seventeen now, a junior, but already he had visited Syracuse and Penn State, and Cornell had as much as promised they'd take him if he could get his grades to an even halfway decent point.

Corky looked at the photos on the wall. Willie scoring this, catching that, Willie on shoulders, Willie held high. "If brains were dynamite you couldn't blow your nose," Corky said to the face on the walls, then ran back to the Charles Atlas ad. *Dare he?*

Corky studied the picture of Mr. Atlas standing there, one perfect arm flexed, modestly smiling by the caption that identified him as "The World's Most Perfectly Developed Man." He read the copy again, about how this incredible being was once actually *ashamed* to strip for sports. "Just watch your scrawny chest and shoulder muscles start to swell . . . those spindly arms and legs of yours bulge."

Corky examined his legs. No doubt about it. Spindly. Thousands were becoming husky. The ad said so. All over America chests were ballooning and here he was, afraid.

Of what?

Of anybody finding out, obviously. Corky looked at the coupon.

CHARLES ATLAS, DEPT 605
115 East 23rd St, N.Y. 10, N.Y.

Send me—absolutely FREE—
a copy of your famous book,
Everlasting Health and Strength,
answers to vital questions and
valuable advice. The book is
mine to keep, and sending it
does not obligate me in any way.

Then it just asked for your name, age and address. Plus you had to mark if you were under fourteen for Booklet A. Corky filled out the coupon, decided Booklet A wasn't for him, didn't check the box, lied, wrote his age as seventeen. He didn't mail the coupon. He put it in an envelope, addressed it, stamped it and stuck it underneath his arithmetic homework in the bottom of his desk.

If it had said anything guaranteeing a plain brown return envelope, he might have sent it off. As it was, he felt like a fool, forgot the whole thing.

Until the Saturday Willie scored three touchdowns against Liberty High giving Normandy its first victory in eleven years. There was honking in the streets that afternoon. And his coupon was in the mail that evening.

Within a week he actually owned *Everlasting Health and Strength.* He grabbed it before anybody else looked at the mail and ferreted it up to his room and lay on his bed and before he read anything, even the letter from Mr. Atlas himself, Corky studied the booklet.

Oh to have a mighty chest. A stomach made of iron. Legs that ran forever. Corky looked at picture after picture of perfection. And all of them, every specimen had once been skinny and beaten, had been saved only by dynamic tension for fifteen minutes a day.

Corky was crushed when he read the letter. It was friendly. It was encouraging. It talked frankly of his problems—Mr. Atlas sensed Corky's growing dissatisfaction with the way he looked.

But the course cost $64.00.

He closed his eyes and lay on his bed. Mutt was right, the Gods pissed on you and that was the way of the world. Not that Mr. Atlas was charging too much—a thousand sixty-four would have been fair to look like you had to look to belong in *Everlasting Health and Strength.*

But he had—he always knew exactly how much money he possessed—one dollar and forty-five cents, period, with no real hope of increasing his fortune till Christmas when Mutt always hit him with a fiver. Briefly, he wondered if his father might lend him his next thirteen Christmases on account, but that was foolish because who had that kind of money.

That night just before he slept, Corky decided that what he needed more than anything else right then was a piece of good news.

It wasn't long in coming. Two weeks was all it took. And it came in the form of a letter from Mr. Atlas himself, nice and chatty, wondering how things were, wondering why he had not received an answer. If it was money, Mr. Atlas went on, that was never a problem. If you were interested in bettering the condition of the human race, money was a secondary motive.

Corky could have the identical course for $48.00.

He almost wrote a thank-you note explaining his position, but he decided that Mr. Atlas was much too busy to read letters from kids, no matter how great their sense of gratitude. Besides, probably his handwriting would give him away. He glanced at *Everlasting Health and Strength* again (it resided beneath his mattress, obvious but safe—no one else made his bed), did a few push-ups, and tried for sleep, deciding that what he really needed more than anything else was a piece of *great* news.

It came two weeks later. Not only was Mr. Atlas lowering his price for the secrets of Dynamic Tension all the way down to its all-time record breaking low of $32.00—*not only that there was more!* Not only would Corky get the identical $64.00 course, if he ordered by return mail he would also get, *at no additional cost whatsoever,* Mr. Atlas' own book on defending yourself against all odds *plus* a photo album portraying *The Greatest Feats of Strength of the Century.*

But this was it, Mr. Atlas said. There would be, if this offer was spurned, no more correspondence between them.

Corky put the letter along with the other two under his mattress. That night at dinner, while Willie and Mutt talked sports, he listened even less than usual. Was he imagining things?

Or was Mr. Atlas getting mad at him.

Two weeks later left no doubt. What is this with you, Mr. Atlas seemed to be thundering. I spend my life getting my system ready so that anybody can have mighty thighs and I offer you a chance and you say no and I offer again and again after that and you still say no? Is money all you care about?

Well it's not all I care about. I care about *you.* And you care about your *body,* or you wouldn't have written in the first place. All right. This is it. The final, final offer.

$16.00.

And because I can tell you're the kind that needs coaxing, here's the deal. You get the $64.00 course. The identical not one syllable changed course. And you still get the pamphlet on defending yourself against all odds, not to mention the photo album of *The Greatest Feats of Strength of the Century.*

But there's more.

The Atlas Secrets of Success with the Opposite Sex is yours free. If you can find it in a bookstore, it's $5.95.

But you get it *free.*

Add it up: *The Atlas Secrets of Success with the Opposite Sex.*

The Greatest Feats of Strength of the Century.
Defending Yourself Against All Odds.

Plus the $64.00 Original Atlas Course in Dynamic Tension.

That is a saving of unparalleled value. Act Today. Offer expires midnight Saturday.

The PS below the signature was when Corky realized genuine fear. It seemed innocuous enough. A simple little additional thought: "If for some reason you cannot accept this offer, perhaps you would feel better if one of our many field representatives called on you."

Corky could not control his heart.

They were coming after him now.

He tried to imagine what a "field representative" for Charles Atlas would look like. A knock at the door. Mutt would answer. A pair of shoulders wider than the frame would be outside. A voice like gravel would ask for a certain seventeen-year-old Charles Withers. Mutt would say, you got it wrong, Corky's not even ten yet.

"Ten!" the field representative would cry. "*Ten?* We been wasting our stamps on a ten-year-old punk? He didn't check that he was under fourteen on the coupon, *that's against the law.*" Maybe Corky didn't know he was doing anything wrong, Mutt would say but now the monster was in the house, roaring. "I DROVE ALL THE WAY UP FROM DEPARTMENT SIX-O-FIVE, ONE HUNDRED FIFTEEN EAST TWENTY-THIRD STREET NEW YORK CITY, WHERE IS HE, WHERE IS THAT LIAR, LET ME GET MY MIGHTY FINGERS ON THAT LYING CHARLES WITHERS."

Corky could not—not—sleep that night till close to morning. He just lay there thinking that he hadn't meant to cause trouble, hadn't wanted any anger, he was just a kid who whittled and one day wondered what it might be like to be strong, please, I'm sorry, just let me alone.

But they wouldn't. Two weeks later: $12.00.

The Charles Atlas organization was after him now. This letter was really angry. Angry and hurt and there would *definitely* be a field representative in the area in the near future.

He hadn't meant to upset anyone. Yes he had lied, sure he had claimed age he hadn't earned yet, but that wasn't worth their anger.

Why were they crucifying him?

Jail? Was that even a remote possibility? Corky could not stop his imagination. At school it was relentless, coming up with torments and humiliations. His mind dogged him day and night; for the first time, school was perplexing, he couldn't concentrate and one of his teachers even admonished him, which had never come close to happening before.

But how could you think about adverbs or percentages when the world's most perfectly developed man was pissed off at you?

He wanted to talk to somebody, anybody, but there wasn't anybody. He knew people; everybody knew people, it wasn't that he was unpopular. But it was hard for him, *people* were hard for him. He was able to stay by himself and he did, he whittled, made figures, dogs and horses and cows and faces and that had been enough to get him through.

All he ever really wanted was to please people. His mother had liked whittling and while she was around that was fine, and after she was gone he kept it up because at least he knew how to do it and do it well.

He began to wonder if they ever came in groups, the Atlas men, traveling in pairs in case they ran into tough customers. Except he wasn't a tough customer, he was just a kid, *leave kids alone.*

When the offer reached $8.00 he waited till very late and then he told his father. Mutt was lying propped in bed watching wrestling on the tube. When Corky started, Mutt's eyes were on the falling figures, but after a while they began flicking back and forth, from his son to the fighters; finally he focused on the boy. "Pal, you gotta watch that imagination of yours."

Corky nodded.

"Quit the crying and listen now."

". . . listening . . ."

"IBM hasn't got that many field representatives, you get me? There's no way some bimbo with muscles is gonna come up here after you, now stop the crying like I said."

". . . they said a man would be in the area . . ."

"Forget what they said, just remember Mutt says don't be afraid. Tell me that."

". . . not afraid . . ."

"And you really mean it?"

Corky decided it would be best to nod.

"Sleep good."

Corky headed for the door.

"Hey Pal? Remember something huh? God gave you the brains. The muscles leave to Willie."

Corky did that very thing till Willie was killed.

Stupidly. Drunkenly. In a car crash. At the age of eighteen. Corky had been having dinner alone with Mutt in front of the tv when the call came. Mutt answered, nodded, muttered a few words, hung up. "They got Willie" was all he said, and Corky knew he was talking of the Gods, they pissed on you, but if you were tough, you survived, and Mutt was tough, he hobbled when he walked, but you didn't mock him about it, and no matter what they did to you, you had to fight back until you died.

Which was why, the week after they put Willie in the ground, Mutt began teaching Corky football . . .

"He's got the good hands, he's got the good speed," Mutt was saying to the coach. "I'm not saying he's another Willie, but the kid can help you, that's a guarantee."

Coach Tyler looked across the field at Corky. It was a steaming August day and Corky stood awkwardly in his brother's old football uniform, holding tight to the helmet. "Not much size," Tyler said.

"Did I say he was big?"

"I don't know, Mutt—he's way behind. We've been working out all summer." He turned, gestured to the rest of the fresh-man team who were running through the heat, getting their wind sprints done.

"I been working with the kid myself, Tyler. I been devoting myself. I would never bring him over if he wasn't ready."

Tyler shrugged. "I owe you, Mutt; what do you want from me?"

"Just a chance for my pal over there."

"As a what?"

"Goddammit, he's got the good speed. He can catch punts, kickoffs, give him a shot."

"Later," Tyler said, and he jogged back to his team.

"Gonna work out just fine for all concerned," Mutt said, coming back to the boy. "Sit awhile." They walked to the old wooden grandstand, took seats alone on the front row. "Still nervous?"

Corky made a nod.

"No one expects miracles."

Corky nodded again.

Mutt watched Tyler with his players. "Best years he ever had he owes to me—I brought him the best, didn't I?"

"Willie was sure wonderful," Corky said.

"He was a pal all right."

"Daddy, I'm not like him."

"No one expects miracles, I said that, just listen to Mutt and that's all you have to do. What are you gonna do when they kick to you?"

"Catch it."

"How come you won't drop it?"

"I'm gonna see the ball into my hands."

"That's all there is to it—*ya see the ball into your hands*—never take your eyes off it no matter what till you got it cradled. Then what do you do?"

"Run fast."

"Why do you think you can do that?"

"'Cause you said I got the good speed."

"And with that good speed, do you run at 'em?"

"No, you juke 'em, you give 'em the leg and then take it away."

"I'm really proud of you," Mutt said.

The heat was terrible and Corky contemplated fainting.

"But that don't matter," Mutt said then.

Corky wondered how much it would hurt, being slammed around. And what did you do with the pain? Where did you put it—you couldn't cry, not on the football field, but the pain had to drain off someplace, where though? I got the good speed, he told himself. Maybe they won't hit me at all. Give 'em the leg, take it away, juke 'em, fake, then run for safety. He looked at Mutt then. "Huh? What do you mean, it doesn't matter if you're proud. I want you to be proud."

"No," Mutt told him. "*You* got to want *you* to be proud. You want me to be pleased, sure; but you're the only one you can be proud of."

"Daddy—listen—please, I don't want to try this—I'm just gonna goof it up—let's go home, maybe there's a baseball game on the tv."

"You got to go through the caldron, Pal. You got to come out the other side. Willie was scared worse than you. And he didn't just have the speed and the hands, he had the size and the strength working for him. And he said over and over again, 'Take me home, Mutt.' Until I told him about Nagurski."

"Nagurski?"

"This was the best thing ever happened to me, the high point of my life, y'understand? And I was there, I saw it all, and I cried, so you pay mind."

Corky stared at his father.

"I've read about 'em all and I've seen 'em all, every man ever run with a football, you name 'em, I made it my business to be there. Only not Nagurski. Bronko Nagurski and they said he was the greatest ever tucked a football under an arm. He was from Minnesota, went to school there, played pro in Chicago, I never got my chance to really check him out. But he was so great that when he wasn't runnin', they couldn't just let him sit on the bench so they played him in the line, played him at tackle, and to this day he is the only one in the history of the world ever made All-American at *two* positions in *one* year—do you realize how great that man must have been? No one else ever dreamed of being All-American at two positions all the same year, and he *done* it. Nagurski. Weighed two thirty-five. Fast they said. Couldn't be brought down, they said. No one ever came close, they said.

"But I never got my shot to really see. I was east and he

was out there. He played pro, tore the league apart, then went
back to Minnesota and I never saw him. Well, you get over
things, I got over that.

"Then one Sunday I was passing through Chicago on my
way back east—I did a lot of truckin' during the war, driving
valuable stuff all over, good work, hard, but it paid, better'n
massagin' I can promise you that, and I read in the papers
that Nagurski was gonna play. Now that wasn't the news. See,
it was wartime, there wasn't enough blue chippers around, so
to fill out the rosters they brought in what they could get, and
I read that Nagurski was coming back, but only to play substi-
tute tackle, not to ever run with the ball.

"But this Sunday in Chicago the papers said maybe, *maybe*
they would have to try to let him run, on account of there was
only three fullbacks and one was injured and another wasn't
up to snuff. So if the half sick one got hurt and his replace-
ment too, well, they had no choice but to give the ball to
Bronko and they asked would he do it if that happened and
he said he didn't much want to but he'd try.

"Fourteen years, Corky. He'd been out of college *fourteen
years*. He'd been retired from the pro game for half that long
and for an athlete, that's seven lifetimes. He was old. *Old* I'm
telling you. And I'm in Chicago, remember, and I'm due back
east, but I thought, I got to see this today, I got to watch,
even if it's a million to one against him ever carrying, I got to
be there if the Bronko gets the ball."

"You said you cried," Corky said.

"I took the bus out to old Commiskey Park. See, this wasn't
just an ordinary game, this was a city rivalry, the Bears
against the Cardinals, and Nagurski, he was with the Bears
and it wasn't even an ordinary city rivalry—the division title
was on the line. The Bears had to win to get to the play-offs.
The Cardinals were dying to stop 'em. This was something—
think of a Normandy-Liberty shoot out and multiply it a hundred times and you got some idea what it was like for the
Bears to be going against the Cardinals, two Chicago teams,
with everything riding. If you'd have given the players lead
pipes, they would have all been dead after the opening

kickoff, that's how hard they hit. And I was there to see it all.

"And the Cardinals slaughtered 'em. Just really took it to 'em. And Nagurski sat on the bench. I tried getting a look at him but I didn't have binocs, he just looked like anybody else. Big, sure, but nothing special, and in the second quarter I think it was, the fullback for the Bears who was feeling poorly, he got racked up bad and he was done and I thought omijesus, am I glad I come to this, there's only one healthy fullback left.

"Then in the third quarter the Cardinals went to town. They were the underdogs, see, but they weren't going to let the Bears go on to glory and when it got to be twenty-four to fourteen with the Cardinals stopping the Bears cold, well, some people even started getting ready to beat the crowd, and the Bears tried a run and the Cardinals wouldn't let nobody go nowhere and everybody unpiled—everybody except the Bears' fullback.

"The whole park knew it, Corky. You could tell. The word was whizzing all around the stands. 'He's comin' in. The Bronko. The Bronko.' And I sat there thinking, omijesus, what a great spot for a legend to be in, coming back after so many years, one quarter to play, the title on the line and ten points behind. You lead your team to victory, you can't ever die after that.

"And then the crowd started screaming like nothin' you ever heard because on the bench, he stood up. Nagurski. And he reached for his helmet. And he come onto the field. And right then as I watched him I knew I was the fool of all the world and if there was one place I didn't want to be it was Commiskey Park in Chicago with Nagurski coming in to play."

"Why, Daddy?"

"Because you could tell when he lumbered on. He was *slow. Fourteen years since college.* Old. Old. It was gone, every bit of what he had was gone, he was nothing, you could see that when he was to the huddle and I knew they were gonna piss on him, they brought him back from Minnesota just so they could piss on him, it didn't matter if he was All-

American at two positions in one year, what matters is how
are you remembered at the end and this was the end but
there was still one chance."

"Tell me, tell me."

"Well, everybody knew they were gonna give the ball to
Bronko but the Bears, they had this Jew quarterback, Luckman, and I don't have to tell you he was smart do I, and if
you're smart and everybody knows what you're gonna do, well
you don't do it, you fake it and do something else and when
they came out of the huddle, and when they lined up with
Nagurski at fullback and Luckman at quarterback, well, it
had to be a decoy thing, they had to pretend to give him the
ball and then Luckman could throw one of his long passes
and maybe the Bears would be only behind by three with a
chance to win it all."

Mutt leaned back against the row behind him and closed
his eyes to the sun.

Corky waited.

"Only it wasn't no decoy."

"You mean they gave him the ball?"

Mutt nodded. "They gave it to him and he put it under his
arm and just kind of ran slow, straight into the Cardinal line.
They were all waiting for him. All these big guys and Nagurski tried, you could see that, but they just picked him up,
the Cardinals did, and for one second they just held him on
their shoulders."

"And then they threw him down?"

"Not exactly, they all fell backwards and he gained four
yards."

"He *gained?*—but you said—"

"—I couldn't believe it either. He kind of got up and shook
himself off and went back into the huddle and out the Bears
come again and this Luckman, he hands the ball to Nagurski
and he lumbers up and they're waiting only this time he falls
forward for eight more. First down."

"How did he do it?"

"I couldn't figure it myself. But it was starting to get a little
eerie on the field. You could see all the Cardinal linemen slap-

ping each other on the asses and the Bears come out again and this time they did fake and the pass was good for another first down and the next play was Nagurski kind of slipping down for six. He was like an ax hitting a tree. It doesn't matter how big the tree is, when the ax starts coming, you better look out.

"Now the Bears were inside the twenty. And there wasn't any doubt about what was gonna happen. It was gonna be the Bronko up the middle and all these Cards, they bunched, waiting, and sure enough, here he comes, and they hit him and he hits them and for a second they did what they could but then he bursts through and he's doing five, six, eight, and then they knock him down and he's crawling—*crawling for the goal*, and everybody's screaming and there's a Cardinal on his back, trying to make him stop but he can't, he can't, and finally about six guys jump him at the one and stop him short of the TD. But they were scared now. They knew he was coming and they knew there wasn't anything they could do about it, and they waved their fists and tried to get steamed up but old Bronko, he just lined up behind the quarterback and the quarterback give him the ball and they're all waiting, Corky—eleven fucking Cards are waiting and this old man starts forward and they're braced and he jumps sideways at them, this old man flies at them and they parted like water and he was through and the rest of the game was nothing, the Bears slaughter them behind the Bronko who gains a hundred yards in one quarter and for a while the Card fans were screaming 'Stop him, *stop him*' but after a little they quit that, nothing could stop him, and after it was over I sat there bawling, and I tried to get at it, what *was* it that had happened out there, because it couldn't happen but it did, *a man pissed back at the Gods*, Corky, and finally I realized you had to be so proud of yourself that nothing else mattered and that's what I taught Willie all those years but not good enough because he got taken, and it's what I'm gonna teach you if you'll listen long enough, and when you go out there today you just think '*I'm* proud of *me I'm* proud of *me*' and then *you'll* be pissing at the Gods and won't that be the day."

Corky did his best, tried very hard, and in the end got both legs broken for the effort.

Not that first scrimmage. He just caught punts then, and he didn't drop any, being careful always to look the ball right into his hands. He caught and he ran but they kept him out of real contact until he knew which way the runbacks went and once he got that straight he did well enough until the second week when he was trying to juke, had his left leg planted in the grass when someone hit him from the side and he could hear something snap and in the pile up it all got very messy, and the other leg got bent the wrong way too, and just before he passed out on the grass, Corky had a moment left to think, and what went through his mind was that he wasn't ever going to have to do this anymore, so all in all, on balance, it was a very lucky day . . .

The magic came out of the pain.

He awoke in Normandy Hospital, a cast from the bottom up. It was dark. Mutt sat in a chair. Corky managed to mutter a few things and his father answered back, but it was impossible to tell who was the more subdued. Finally Mutt looked at his watch. "Gotta go give massages," he said.

Corky nodded.

"Want me to bring anything?"

Corky couldn't think.

"Whittling stuff?"

Corky shook his head. "Too messy. The shavings."

"Get some sleep, Pal," Mutt said.

Corky did as he was told.

He awoke several hours later, feeling better and bored. He asked a nurse for something. She brought him what she called the game box, but it was only a dirty deck of cards, a pair of dice and a lotto board. He asked for something to read. She brought a pile of magazines, left him. Corky thumbed through. Comics. Romance magazines.

And *Classy Classics Volume I* by Merlin, Jr.

Card tricks? Corky studied the faded pamphlet, almost put it down, didn't. He opened it instead, read page one:

All magic, it goes without saying,
is illusion. The *effect* of the
illusion is how it appears to the
audience. The *preparation*
for the illusion is everything—
from the crimping of a card
to the practicing of ten thousand hours. If the preparation has been sufficient and
proper, then the execution
of the illusion is inexorable:
before you're even started,
the work is done.

By the great ones, and I would
be lying if I didn't include
myself, magic is the ultimate
entertainment: they, the audience, will never forget you,
or hold you less than kindly in
their hearts. What I'm saying, all
you beginners out there, is this:
you do it right, they can't love
you enough . . .

Corky reached into the game box, took out the dirty deck of playing cards. He squeezed them a few times, bent them one way, then the other. They felt okay. But then, he always did have the good hands.

And the good speed didn't matter anymore.

PEG

He wasn't sure she even knew his name until the afternoon she called out "Corky, can we talk?" He was leaving high school for the day, walking down the front steps; she was at the bottom, surrounded as always by boys. It was early April, only starting to warm, and she was in her plaid skirt and the white sweater plus the oxblood loafers with the dimes.

It wasn't one of her best days, she looked barely perfect. With the dark blonde hair and the dark blue eyes and the incredible this and the glorious that that could drive you crazy if you thought about it long enough.

Pointless going on. You could not, Corky realized months ago at the start of freshman year, explain the impact of Peggy Ann Snow by talking about specifics.

He used to spend a lot of time figuring how to best impress her. He rescued her from burning buildings and runaway cars. He fought thieves and rapists, not to mention smugglers and spies, though why the spies were after her he never quite worked out, or, for that matter, what it was the smugglers wanted up in the Catskills. But that was the thing about Peggy Ann Snow. She put weird thoughts in your head.

And they didn't go away.

"Corky, can we talk?"

He stopped where he was on the steps, watched as she left the group of junior boys, hurried over to him. "I guess we've never really met, I'm Peggy Snow, you're Corky."

Nod.

"Hi."

He gave a kind of small, casual wave.

"I hear you do . . ." and she mimed something, probably pulling a rabbit out of a hat ". . . stuff."

Nod.

"Listen, I'm facing a real problem and it would mean just the world to me if you'd kind of help out."

"Depends."

"See, Lucas—that's my twerp of a kid brother—Lucas is having an eighth birthday a week from Saturday and Mom said it was time I pulled my weight so she's cooking but I have to handle keeping them quiet. So if I paid you, would you do a magic show?"

"Never done one."

"I can spring for two dollars."

"It's time for my debut."

Not much of a line but it made her smile.

Ahhhhhh.

He spent the intervening days working out his routine. Start with the flashy stuff or save those for the end? If you started big, you could lose interest before you were half done. If you started small, you might never *get* half done. Corky did a lot of listmaking. Probably eight-year-olds were a tough audience so what he decided to do was *only* flashy stuff, one climax to another, constantly knocking them dead.

Peg introduced him.

Corky stood behind the pinned up sheet in the basement of her house by Lake Melody. He was wearing his top hat and magician's cape and carrying his wand and he listened to the commotion out front as the dozen kids got seated. And suddenly, it was very hard to breathe. He inhaled a few times, cleared his throat. Ahead of him Peg went, "*Say hello to Corky Withers,*" unpinned the sheet, and he was on.

"*Mam-zelle,*" he said and bowed to Peggy. He smiled at the children. "*Mes amis.*"

"Why is he talking that way?" one of the kids in the middle front said.

"Shut up, Lucas," Peggy said. "He's a great French magician."

"I thought he went to school right here."

"He happens to now," Peggy answered, "but he's spent a *lot* of time in France, so just zip it up, Lucas."

Corky brought out two billiard balls from his cape and held them high. "'ooo would like to play zee beel-yards? Eet is impossible, *non? Parce que* zere are needed three balls for to play zee beel-yards. *Voilà!*" Corky made a big gesture with his left hand and while they followed that, he pushed the billiard ball shell into position with his thumb so that when he held his right hand high, it looked like there were three balls now.

"Terrific," Peggy said, leading the applause, or doing her best to, because no one else did any clapping.

"I got that trick, it's a shell," the one next to Lucas said.

"*Mais non,*" Corky got out.

"Then throw us the three balls," Lucas said.

"Fat lip time is coming up," Peggy said. "Anybody interested?"

Corky got out the disappearing cigar. "When someone try to smoke in mah pre-zahnce, I am poo-lite. I ask, *s'il vous plaît,* out wiz zee see-gar. Eef zay say *oui,* I do nozzing. Eef zay say *non—*" and he clapped his hands together, raising the right one higher, the one with the cigar, because that activated the gimmick on his inside sleeve and pulled the cigar up and out of sight. You had to do it just right to give the impression of disappearance with any skill at all, and Corky knew as he made the move that he'd never done it better. Peggy clapped. Corky bowed.

Lucas farted.

Uproar. Shrieks and screams and when Corky tried to begin the mystery of the bottomless milk pitcher there was no way of being heard, and he tried going on until Lucas belched and that set off a chain belch reaction that went on until Peg struck like an avenging angel, grabbing her brother by the neck, dragging him up to the stage crying, "Get the stuff Corky—*now,*" but Corky didn't get it and Peg said, "The *French* stuff for God's sakes, the stuff you demonstrated in science class, the stuff that *freezes your tongue to the roof of your mouth*" and now Corky managed, "The French freezing stuff, right," and as he started off Lucas was screaming,

"Don't do it—don't freeze my tongue" but Peg was having none of it, saying, "It only lasts an hour, you'll love it" and then Lucas was going, "I'll be so quiet, I will I will, gimme a chance *please!*" Eventually Peg relented.

And the rest of the performance went wonderfully well.

"Sorry it couldn't be more," Peg said, when it was over, the basement quiet now, the children upstairs eating. She handed him the two dollars.

Corky shook his head "no."

"C'mon, a deal's a deal."

"Please."

She looked at him. "Hey you mean it."

Nod.

"How come you're so quiet?"

Shrug.

"Boy, you're just as weird as they say—"

"—who says I'm weird?—"

"Gotcha that time." She smiled. "Nobody. I was only trying to get a rise out of you."

"Do people?" he wondered, since it was something he suspected all along to be true.

"You are awful quiet, Corky."

"Nothing much to say."

"Okay." She helped him gather up his tricks and boxes, put them into a shopping bag so they'd fit neatly. Then she walked him to his bicycle. "Bye, Corky, thanks."

He nodded, started riding off.

"And you're good," she shouted after him.

"Gonna be," he shouted back. "Someday . . ."

After that they always nodded in the halls, and if there was anything to talk about, spoke. He helped her with her homework sometimes—she spelled atrociously—and tried to make himself, unobtrusively, handy, and there were times when he was almost positive she liked him.

That summer Mutt got him a job chopping lettuce at the G. A thousand guests a night, salads twice a day, it made for a

busy summer. He made up his poem at the start of the second
week to stop from going mad.

> . . . Peggy Ann Snow
> Peggy Ann Snow
> Please let me follow
> Wherever you go . . .

It wasn't much of a poem really, but then he never fancied
himself to be a poet. And regardless of its merits, it was a lot
better than others he tried.

> . . . Beautiful Peg
> Beautiful Peg
> Don't go away and forget me
> I beg . . .

P. B. Shelley didn't have a lot to worry about . . .

It was natural that, sooner or later, she would take up with
Ronnie Wayne and that fall, she did. Corky wasn't even jealous, that's how natural it was; Ronnie Wayne had it all. His
nickname was "Duke" and he was a senior and he had his
own car, a convertible. That was nothing. His father ran the
most successful real estate operation in Normandy. Still nothing. Ronnie "the Duke" got decent grades in school without
cracking a book, he could shoot pool better than the poor
kids, he was more popular than any other senior but best of
all, at that time, in the year of our Lord 1959, he looked
shockingly like Elvis Presley.

"Withers," he whispered one autumn day. "Take this to
Stuck-up."

"Who?" They were in the school library, study hall, everyone in their own seat and no moving around, a rule that didn't
apply to Corky, since he worked in the library for extra
money and besides, Miss Beckmire, the librarian, liked him,
probably because he had a sweet face and was always polite
and could read faster than anybody else in Normandy High.

Duke held out the note for Corky. "Snow, for chrissakes."

Corky took the folded paper and strolled the length of the enormous room, dropped it on Peggy's desk. "From the Duke," he whispered.

Peggy unfolded the note, read it, then got out her pencil and scribbled a reply on a sheet of paper of her own. She stopped in the middle, whispered, "Is conceited i-e or e-i?" He told her, she finished the note, folded it, and he took it back to Duke.

There were three complete exchanges that study period, three again the next day, culminating in Duke taking Peggy out for Cokes after school. Corky stood by his bicycle and watched the parking lot as Duke tore out toward town. The top was down. Peggy's dark blonde hair was blowing. Corky felt, no question about it, really good about the whole thing.

Peggy's right, you are weird, he told himself.

And peddled home.

He passed notes between the two of them for all that week and well into the next, and if Miss Beckmire suspected, she didn't do anything. And the second Wednesday, Peggy invited Corky to come along.

They went to The Hut, which was only the biggest and busiest place in town as far as the high school was concerned, and they had Cokes and Duke ordered a plate of crisp fries and they devoured them so fast Duke had to order another.

Corky sat there, trying to not look impressed. But it was hard. My God, why shouldn't it be, you're sitting between the prettiest girl and the most popular boy and *they invited you*.

They did it several more times that October and afterwards, Corky made quick notes when he got home, because probably he had never had better times than those and you never knew how long they'd last.

Mutt got fired before Thanksgiving. He'd been becoming increasingly morose ever since Willie's crash, and one day he just slugged the head of the gym at Grossinger's and wised off to a couple of the customers who tried to intervene, and you didn't do that kind of thing and expect to stick around.

He lucked out though, latched onto an opening at a private club in Chicago near the Loop, and it was amazing, after living all those years in one place, how fast you could leave when there was nothing holding you back.

His last day at school, Corky went to Peg's house to say good-bye, and give her a wooden heart he'd whittled but it was cheerleading practice afternoon, so he went to the girls' gym and waited outside. It was after four when he got there and after five when the first girl left.

It wasn't Peggy.

Corky waited. It was getting cold now. Inside the lit building he could hear the cheers going on over and over, getting perfect so that the Normandy Tigers might somehow beat the Liberty Wildcats in the final grudge game of the season. The darkening afternoon was filled with strident voices:

> Look out (clap-clap-double clap)
> Here we come
> We've got those Wildcats on the run.
> So
> Look out Wildcats (double clap twice)
> The Tigers (clap)
> The Tigers have (clap-clap)
> CLAWS.
> (hey-hey)

Corky walked around the front of the building awhile, always glancing back to the door, checking to see no one came out. The wooden heart was burning in his hand now. It was stupid. Making it was stupid, waiting was stupid.

No one came out.

Five-twenty.

Five-forty-five was when he took the heart, threw it as far as he could, away for now and ever.

Going on six.

> Look out (clap-clap-double clap)
> Here we come
> We've got those Wildcats on the run.

So
Look out Wildcats (double clap twice)
The Tigers (clap)
The Tigers have (clap-clap)
CLAWS.
(hey-hey)

"Corky?"

"That you, Peg?" He sauntered over in the dark, smiled at her. "Boy am I ever lucky, running into you."

They started away from the gym.

"What are you doing?" he asked.

"Cheerleading practice."

Corky nodded. "Well I'm sure glad I got the chance."

"Chance?"

"Family's kind of heading on. Mutt got a big break in Chicago."

Her turn to nod.

He could tell from the way she did it that she knew. "You heard I guess."

"About the thing at Grossinger's? I'm really sorry."

"Well, he's a scratchy guy, it was bound to happen."

"I'm still sorry."

"So I'll see you, Peg."

She started away.

He watched in silence.

She said "oh" out loud then, and spun in the night, running into his arms. "I just realized something awful."

"What?"

"I'll miss you." They stood like that awhile.

(hey-hey)

MERLIN

The giant kept falling up the stairs. He would land hard, sit puffing, rise, try another step or two, then his balance would go and he would fall again. He never lost his temper, didn't seem to mind the time the trip to the second floor landing took. It was as if the only way to make it was up, then down, gather strength, then onward and upward again.

Scared, Corky watched from the second floor shadows.

The giant made it to the top step, panted awhile. Then he reached an enormous hand into a jacket pocket, fumbled around. The hand eventually came out empty. Now it was the turn of the other hand to try the left jacket pocket. Empty. "Fug," the giant said. Then he grabbed hold of the top of the banister, stood. His right hand tried his pants pocket and the giant soon nodded, took out a key, lurched to the nearest doorway, pushed the key in the lock. Or at least that was the theory. He missed again and again, sometimes coming closer to the keyhole, never close enough to attempt insertion. The key slipped from his fingers and bounced along the floor. The giant bent for it, a mistake, tumbled down hard, lay there.

"Don't worry, Mr. Merlin," Corky said, and he dashed out of the shadows, picked up the key, unlocked the door, helped Merlin up, guided him inside, found a wall light, flicked it on, moved the slumping giant to the sofa, went back, flicked the room to darkness.

The giant awoke hours later, parched. He made it to his feet, made it to the kitchen, got a glass, drank. Then he returned to the couch and closed his eyes.

"Would you like me to make you some coffee?"

On went the couch lamp. The giant looked at the kid. "How'd you get in here?"

"I brought you in here."

"Oh."

"Maybe an Alka-Seltzer? I could run out and try and find a drugstore. Someplace is sure to be open."

"What are you, some kid genie?"

"Nossir, my name's Corky Withers and I want to be a great magician like you."

"A dumb genie, just my luck," Merlin said. Off went the couch light and he slept.

When he awoke next it was late morning and breakfast was ready. Coffee and toast anyway. Merlin sipped the dark liquid. "Okay, down to cases, what's all this?"

"Nothing. Only what I told you already. I want them to never forget me. I want them to hold me kindly in their hearts."

"Where'd you hear that shit?" Merlin wanted to know.

"You *wrote* it. *Classy Classics Volume I*. I've got the whole series, all four pamphlets."

"Supposed to be twenty. Fugging publisher skipped on me." Merlin shook his head. "I'm not up to private students anymore. Usually all you get is bimbo psychiatrists who use it for therapy."

"You don't understand, Mr. Merlin. I've got to be great. I'm very good now. Better than practically anybody. But I'm not great yet. That's why I've come to you."

"You do close-up magic?"

"Yessir."

"Do me something."

Corky got out a quarter, put it in his right hand, thumb palmed it, closed both hands, blew on them, opened his hands empty.

"Shitty," Merlin, Jr. said.

"When you say shitty, you don't mean shitty, you mean not great, right?"

"I never saw a worse thumb palm. You're an amateur, kid. Who'd you study with?"

"Books mostly."

"Do a drop vanish."

Corky did one.

Merlin just looked at him.

"Shitty?"

Merlin nodded.

"Cards are more my specialty."

"Amaze me."

Corky pulled his pack of bicycles from his Windbreaker jacket, held them out. "Want to examine them?"

"Get to it."

"Okay, do you know Paul Le Paul's Double Deuce?"

"Get to it I said."

"Ordinary deck. I'll shuffle the cards." Corky did a faro shuffle, followed up with the Hindu.

"Shitty."

"I didn't do the trick yet."

"And you're not gonna, not for me, I got a weak stomach."

"I'm not that bad."

"I'm sorry kid; y'are."

Corky put his cards away in his Windbreaker jacket.

"What's your name again?"

"Corky Withers."

"Withers—look around you. This pit is my home. The Collier Brothers would be happy here, but I'm not."

Corky glanced around. It was a small apartment, living room, a bedroom, kitchenette and bath. And crammed. Corky had never seen so much magic apparatus in his life. There were shelves full of magic books, boxes piled all over. Vent dolls and egg bags and top hats and gimmicks, fakes and pulls, escape boxes, silks of every color and size.

Corky thought it was kind of terrific.

"Magic's on the skids, Withers. Before my dumpling died last year—" he pointed to a photo of a round, smiling woman "—we had to travel ten months a year to survive. Ten years ago we had to travel four. Once I could stay right here in Los Angeles and eat steak whenever. So what I'm telling you, kid, is why not get yourself an Edsel franchise, you'll do a lot better. Corner the market in cable cars, if you want. But ride clear of this."

Corky shook his head.

"I'm talking to you 'cause you're a handsome kid, you got a sweet look, you made me coffee. I'm leveling, believe that. I, Hymie Merlin, Jr., am as good as the game. That's no shit gospel. I been forty-two out of fifty years in magic. And why have I failed?"

"You haven't failed."

"I'll trade you bank accounts blind, the Rockefellers wouldn't make you that offer. Why is because of what magic is and that's one thing and one thing only: *entertainment.* Why can't I entertain? I'm charming, I got good patter, the magic's as good as the game."

"I don't know."

"Take a peek at my face, Withers."

Corky looked at the huge nose and the wide eyes and the wild hair and the bad mouth with one corner always turned down.

"I'm ugly, Withers; I got a puss stops clocks. I can't get on the tv, I can't do schtick with kids, I survive on a limited market. Now, how do we know that if you get great like me, if you spend those *years,* maybe you won't be ugly but maybe you won't have charm. Maybe you'll eat your guts out seeing guys who can't do shit getting all the marbles 'cause they got charm. You got charm, Withers?"

"Nossir."

"Then good-bye."

"I came to you because it began with you but there's a million others. *You can't stop me.*"

"I'm just trying—"

"—*I've-got-to-do-this-thing!*"

Merlin looked across. "Hey, you're crazy, aren't you, Withers?"

". . . yessir . . ."

"How old?"

"Be nineteen."

"How much you got; I cost."

"Three thousand dollars."

"From what?"

"My dad helped run a health club in San Diego the last couple years. It's his life insurance money."

"We'd have to start from the top, unlearn all the shit you picked up."

"I'm a terrific learner."

"You also thought you were a terrific magician."

"Okay I'm a shitty learner."

A nod from the giant. "You just started learning."

Lesson number one was holding cards in your hands. That was all. Corky couldn't believe it. But those were the instructions. You went to sleep with a pack of cards in each hand and you woke up that way and when you took the bus, you carried the cards and you carried them to the cafeteria, putting them down when you ate but that was all, and in the movies you carried them and ran your fingers along the edges, getting the feel, getting the feel, you weren't going no place until you had that feel, and Merlin told of Baker, the Princeton kid who was the greatest hockey player of them all and how he used to flash across the rink in total darkness, guiding the puck blind, because if you had to look for it, if you didn't feel without seeing, forget it.

Merlin lived in what the real estate people called an "interesting" area between Wilshire and Pico near Fairfax, but what it really was, was a slum on the make, though there were still enough old Jews and aspiring blacks and musicians and artists to make it bearable. Corky took a room at the nearest Y and bought a small mirror and a close-up pad, a thin sponge, and he sat and stared at his hands in the mirror holding the cards and when lesson numbers two and three came, they came together, strengthening the ring and the pinkie. You needed the one strong for dealing bottoms and the other for any kind of decent pass and Merlin said that with most, the thumb was too strong if anything, the index and middles strong enough. But the ring and the pinkie were problems, especially with the left hand and both hands had to be the same if you wanted to be great, so Corky sat in front of his small mirror in his Y room and he did lifts with his pinkie, stretches with his ring, then reversed the procedures, over and over till his fingers started cramping. That was good, Merlin said, the cramping showed you were serious but you had to wash your hands awhile then, get them warm so the muscles would stop their rebellion.

Then back to the mirror, back to the mirror, you had to get the pinkie strong, look out for the ring, work the pinkie, work the ring, forget the cramping, keep at it, keep at it, you had to keep at it if you wanted to be great.

Merlin was great. Corky could tell that the second week of his apprenticeship when the giant brought him along to an Elks' smoker in the Valley and Merlin did his close-up stuff, an escape or two, some terrific silk changes, but the audience liked it better when he talked. Merlin made terrible jokes about always getting mistaken for Cary Grant—his jokes seemed mostly to kid about his beauty—and they gave him a decent enough round of applause before they went back to their serious drinking and Merlin picked up fifty in cash from the chief honcho, then drove Corky back to the Y, on the way asking what he thought of the first Cary Grant joke and Corky said fine, why, and Merlin said I was covering a mistake, you always got to have something ready, Leipzig made mistakes, I make mistakes, remember the knife throwing story and Corky asked what that was and Merlin said it was from a play where an actor had to throw a knife at a wall and what the actor said was, if the knife stuck, "I'm the best in town" and if he missed he said, "I used to be the best in town." Remember that advice, and Corky said he would and when they were at the Y Merlin said, get lots of sleep, tomorrow we begin with the palm.

There are coin palms and card palms. For coins you had to know the classic and the edge and the thumb, those were crucial, but the back palm and the back thumb palm were handy to have around too. For cards, you weren't going anywhere without the diagonal palm and the swing palm, the top, the flip over, the crossways and the bottom.

When you went on in coins you had to get your switches and your flips and then all the vanishes. Cards had a different world of sleights: lifts and deals, shuffles, slips and, naturally, the passes.

Corky was good inside a year, good but not, no one needed to tell him, great, and his money was gone but that wasn't as tragic as it might have been since Merlin had a little stroke after the tenth month and Corky moved in with the giant for what at first was going to be temporary, tending him, sleeping on the couch, talking magic, working magic, reading reading reading the bookshelves through, and when Merlin was around and active he liked the company, he'd always had it, he'd married the dumpling when he was still in his teens. So Corky stayed, and drove the old man's station wagon to jobs, assisted with the act, and when it came time for the major swings up along the coast, Corky chauffeured and watched and packed and learned, when he wasn't quite twenty, that he was, astonishingly, good at picking up girls in bars, secretaries and stews and clerks, and at first he thought it was some kind of fluke streak he was riding, but eventually he realized it had to do with a pleasing impression, that's what they said mostly, he seemed to be nice.

He hoped they were right, thought they were too. And prayed fervently that they never changed their minds.

He and Merlin moved all across the West, Nevada, Colorado, every place big enough to have an order of Elks or some Freemasons, Lion's Clubs, Knights of Columbus, Pythian Sisters. They went to cocktail parties in Seattle, fund raisers in Ashland, Oregon; trade shows, women's clubs, sales meetings, and between jobs, Corky sat by his mirror and worked, improving his forces, getting the estimations down, flourishes of all kinds, many his own. He was starting to invent his own moves now, maybe not better but different from before, things that never existed were starting to flock to him.

Once that started, Merlin pointed out the Stardust.

"What's that?" Corky asked. They were seated in the wagon, driving home after a tough time in Santa Monica.

Merlin was aging badly. The Cary Grant jokes were carrying him now.

"Club."

"So?"

"It's a regular nightclub. Sophisticated. But for you, special."

"I don't think I'm gonna like this," Corky said.

"You're getting very good, Corky."

"But?"

"No. You are. It's time you went out on your own."

"I knew I wasn't going to like it."

"You never yet performed in all your life alone."

"I'm not ready."

"You're going to have to face it someday. I don't mean helping me set up either. I mean going out alone on a stage. You against them and you come out champeen. It's time."

"No it isn't."

"How old are you please?"

"What difference does it make, I'm not ready."

"You're goddam near twenty-six and you are ready. This place"—he gestured to the Stardust—"it's perfect for you. Mondays *anyone* performs. No pressure. You just sign up early enough and the first couple dozen do an act. Sing, tell jokes. They never get magicians hardly. You'd be a novelty. I know they'd take to you."

Corky shook his head.

"You're not skyrocketing with me exactly."

"I'm learning."

"Learned."

"Let's go home."

Merlin started the car. "What are you afraid of?"

"I'm not afraid, I'm just not great yet."

"Remember what I said that first day?"

"That I was crazy, you mean?"

Merlin nodded. "Don't let me turn out to be right."

The next weeks Merlin's work took another drop, and he raised Corky from a 10 to 25 percent partner. Corky wasn't doing any performing, but everything else was his responsibility now. Pinning the gimmicks into just the right places on Merlin's magic suit. (He couldn't do straight close-up anymore, only stuff with gimmicks and fakes.) Making the bookings, driving the car, setting up the act in its entirety. Merlin got more reflective, going back a lot to when he worked with Cardini getting equal billing, how he stumped Thurston once with a sleight of his own that he worked into The Miser's Dream. How he, the last week his wife was alive, spent all the time with her in the hospital, got so he could catch her thoughts.

Corky didn't know what was true or wasn't, but on general principle, he believed it all.

They went, to humor the old man, to the Stardust on a Monday, sitting in the back, watching the entire three hour show. The owner-MC intoduced the acts, explained that none of them had ever performed before—"and if we're lucky won't ever perform again" somebody shouted from the audience but the MC shut him up with "I thought they got you last week for child molesting" and there was laughter and some applause.

Then the talent started. The MC read each name out from a card, giving an intro the performer had written himself. Then the MC went to a corner table, took a big hourglass, and turned it upside down. "You're on," he said as the hourglass touched the table, and the first talent jumped onto the stage, nodded, bowed, quickly turned on a small tape recorder, made sure it was going, faced the crowd again and said, "I don't want to say that my wife's a rotten cook or anything but last night she woke me and said, 'Herbie, Herbie, I think there's thieves in the kitchen, I think they're eating the pot roast I made tonight' and I said, 'Go back to sleep, what do we care, as long as they don't die in the house.'"

He was the best comedian.

He was followed by a lit major from UCLA who froze halfway through her Ronald Reagan imitation. After that came a young man who sang, a cappella, 'What Kind of Fool Am I?', two middle-aged men who played harmonica duets, a black comedian who said "motherfucker" constantly, three black high school girls who tried the Supremes, a piano player/composer/comic who sang his own ballad called "Charles Manson Was a Good Dancer" plus a lot of other people who wanted to be Bob Dylan, Woody Allen and Lenny Bruce.

When it was over, Merlin just said, "Bullshit you're not ready."

Corky had nothing to reply.

But from then on, he really started to work. He sat silently in his room hour after hour, studying his hands in the mirror, producing aces, putting cards into the middle of the deck only to have them instantly appear on the bottom, then they were back in the middle, then they jumped to the top. He dealt seconds for hours on end, taking the next to the top card perfectly, and Merlin watched him once and no one knows how hard dealing seconds is except another magician and Merlin, *Merlin* said out loud, "Head of the fugging class."

Corky began polishing his spring flourishes, sending the cards flying from one hand to another, then the drop flourish, the cards almost reaching the floor. He did one hand cuts and double cuts and false cuts and triple lifts, which are extraordinarily hard, where you lift the top card only you don't, you take three and hold the three out pretending they're only one and when he had that pat he did the quadruple lift which is that much harder because when you have four cards held out, they have bulk, they seem thick, and it becomes almost impossible to handle them as one card unless your hands are extraordinarily graceful.

Corky's hands were that, even on bad days.

Merlin's days got better, strength returned in partial quantity, they did another hop skip and jump tour up the coast, to Portland and back, touching base with all the Elks and Lions and any Rotarian order of *any* persuasion that had even the tiniest entertainment budget, and when they returned to Merlin's L.A. home it was the holiday season, party time, and he did a lot of private shindigs, sometimes mingling with the guests, usually standing at the end of some room or other, telling his Cary Grant jokes, doing his routines, like The Miser's Dream, a favorite of his and a classic piece of business where the magician asks for a hat from the audience and it's empty and his sleeves are empty but then wham—wham—he's producing coins from the air, six, eight, a dozen half dollars, and the way Merlin worked the trick, he had the halves pinned to the inside of his magic suit and Corky placed the money in piles of four so that Merlin could misdirect with the hat, flick one of his giant hands to the familiar spot, pull out four more coins, on and on until the audience, if he did it right, applauded spontaneously, and now he had fourteen and now sixteen and he misdirected with the hat, waving it up and jingling it and the audience watched the hat as they were supposed to and Merlin's right hand stopped working, he tried another grab, no good, and Corky was running forward from his place in the corner of the room before the old man really started to drop completely and his right leg was giving on him and all he said was "I must be getting old" before Corky grabbed him, stopping his crumple midway.

Merlin finished his fall the following Tuesday when they put him in the ground.

"You got till the end of the month," the landlady said to Corky, who nodded. They were standing in front of Merlin's apartment, the day after the burial. "If you want to keep it, I don't mind that if you pay."

"No money."

"Till the end of the month, then," she said, and went back upstairs where she lived. Corky watched her go. Ten days wasn't a whole lot of time.

Except that one of them was a Monday.

He went to the Stardust that very night and asked for the owner. Eventually the guy came out. Corky recognized him from when they had been there a year ago; his beard was grayer now.

"It's about the amateur night," Corky said.

"That's Monday."

"I know. But I'd like to put my name down now. Corky Withers."

"We don't work it that way—you show up Monday afternoon after four—the first two dozen are it. All very American."

"How early do I have to be here to be sure to get on do you think?"

Shrug. "Depends."

"I mean, is it better to go first or in the middle or at the end do you think?"

"Depends."

"Are there ever people here to see you? I mean, if somebody was terrific, would there ever be maybe an agent or manager or like that do you think?" and before the guy could shrug or speak, Corky said, "Depends."

The manager looked at him. "You don't wanna make the audience nervous, y'know."

"Oh I would never do that."

"Yeah?—well you're making me nervous right now."

"Monday," Corky said. The manager started to leave him. He glanced in at the stage. Business wasn't much. "One last thing? If someone, say, comes on a Monday and is, for example maybe terrific, would you hire him to work here regular?"

"Once that should only happen," the manager said.

Corky ran back to his cards. Five minutes wasn't much time, so you had to program it right. Start off easy, end big, but always leave a little something in reserve. If they wanted an encore you had to have a topper so—

An encore?

Just get though it, jerk; just do it right, so they'll never forget you and always hold you kind in their hearts.

Do it right.

Do it right.

Corky put in sixteen hours on Wednesday before he broke, walked around the block a little, napped, made some coffee, got back to it. Another eight hours was plenty, didn't want to empty the gas tank before the race started. Again he napped, a good one. Friday another eight on, four off, eight on, then Saturday he hit it big, staying glued to his mirror, watching his hands, looking for the least clue that might blow it for an audience.

Do it right.

Do it right.

Sunday he began to taper off. Don't leave your fight in the gym. He had his routine down so that depending on applause (if he got applause—thinking about applause was maybe even a little less helpful than worrying over encores) it would run four minutes thirty to four-fifty-five. No point in stretching for the full five or running over. If it only took four-ten, that wasn't gonna hurt either. Don't push. Always leave 'em laughing. Less is more.

He got to the Stardust at eleven Monday morning.

It didn't open till four.

He laughed out loud. A good sign. He hadn't panicked or berated himself. He thought about going back to his mirror, working some more but enough was enough, he'd done his eighty hours for the week, better to take your mind away.

A James Bond double feature was playing in the area, and that seemed just about perfect. He checked the time when he went in, saw that if he stayed for both features he'd be cutting it a little close, so he stayed for the first and half the second and got back to the Stardust at quarter of four.

Thirty people in line.

Please, no!

He counted again. Thirty—wait though—a bunch of them were talking—they knew each other—moral support—and one bunch of four looked like a group of some kind—it was gonna be fine, it was, it was, he'd worked too hard for it not to be.

He was given number twelve. The bearded manager remembered him. "I don't know if it's a good position or not," he said.

"Depends I guess," Corky answered. Then: "What happens now?"

"Fill out the card—name—address if you want—agent if you got one—and how you want me to introduce you. Put that part in quotes. Then you're on your own."

Corky nodded, wrote an introduction on a card, handed the card to the manager. The manager gave him a number. A red plastic 12. "I'll call your number and you come on. Be here by eight-thirty, show starts at nine."

Corky went back to Merlin's place. A nap would have

helped but too risky, what if he overslept, beat himself that way.

In the end he just sat there for two hours. Then he cleaned up, changed—he'd long ago decided not to wear anything fancy. Of course, he didn't *own* anything fancy which made the decision a lot easier. Gray slacks and a white shirt and gray cardigan sweater. Casual. No mumbo jumbo crap. A pack of bicycles in each pocket and scoot.

He didn't start getting unpleasantly nervous until he reached the Stardust. He was there at 8:30 on the money, but in order to make that work he'd had to take a twenty-minute stroll around the area. Still, he wasn't the first. The performers bunched outside in the bar area. In the middle was the desk with the entrance to the club. The manager waited there, escorting people to their tables. It was going to be jammed, one of the girl performers said.

Good or bad, Corky wondered, then decided, didn't matter, nothing like that mattered.

Do it right.

Do it right.

What's your act? another girl asked a curly headed boy. Nostalgia, I imitate Mort Sahl was the reply.

I wonder if he's good, Corky thought. If he is, I wonder if he's before me. And if he's good and if he's before me, is that good?

It doesn't goddammit matter. What *you* do matters. That's it. It's on *your* shoulders. No excuses. You've spent the time, you know the moves.

—quit making me nervous—

The show started promptly which was a surprise. The first performer never showed. Panic. Neither did the third. Same. The second sang the "Age of Aquarius" and the fourth did comedy birdcalls.

Christ I wish that guy was just ahead of me, Corky thought. After this is over I'm gonna hire that birdcall guy and have him come on before me all over the country.

The black girl that was five was funny.

So was the white guy that was sixth.

The seventh person carried a box on stage and for one minute of blind horror Corky thought he was another magician, but that was just nerves, imagination, the guy was a singer and the box held his tape recorder.

Number eight. Now nine. The acts were beginning to blend on him.

Ten didn't show.

Nor eleven.

"Say hello to Corky Withers," the MC read.

Corky walked through the room toward the stage. All he heard were couples ordering drinks from waiters but that was imagination. Maybe one guy ordering one Scotch, rocks, no big deal. He stepped onto the stage. People were all around him, very close.

He blinked from the lights. He hadn't expected the lights. No. He knew they were there, just not so bright. He hadn't expected the heat. They'll think it's nerves, he realized, and it's not, I'm fine, I was a fool to wear the sweater.

"Ordinary cards," he began. "See?" He took one pack, pulled the cards out, handed them to a pretty girl at a ringside table. She showed them to her date.

Somebody coughed.

Corky took the cards back, riffled through. "Now I'd like you to pick one," he said to the pretty girl, and he used the Annemann Force, doing it perfectly, so that when she took the king of spades she had no idea he had made her do it. "And you sir," Corky said to her date, doing Can den Bark's Force on the guy, so in case anyone was watching close for him to repeat himself, they'd never catch him. The guy picked the heart queen—it was amazing the way that worked, women picking kings and men the other way. But it did.

It was very quiet.

"Show the room your card please," Corky said to the pretty girl.

She did.

"Can't see," somebody called.

"Too dark," from somewhere else.

"It's the king of spades," Corky said. "And his is the queen of hearts."

"He got it right," the girl said to the room.

"Mine too," her date said.

He moved to the next two tables, gave each a deck of cards. "Please make a cut into two piles," he said to them. "Then hold the piles up."

When the four piles were held Corky wondered if he'd made a mistake—estimation was one of his strengths, but if you even missed a little, you blew it from the audience's point of view. If you hit it, though, you had them. He took a breath, concentrated, then pointed to the four piles in turn. "Seventeen. Thirty-five. Twenty. Thirty-two. Would you each please count your piles and tell me how many you have. Thank you." They nodded, started to count.

Corky stood there.

"Five, six, seven," one of the women said half aloud.

"Shhh," her date said, "I forgot where I was."

Corky stood there sweating. *Why were they counting so slowly?*

Silence.

"Um-hmm," the first counter done said. "Twenty is the answer."

"Thirty-two here."

"Thirty-five."

"Seventeen."

Corky took the cards back, waited for some applause.

Still the silence.

He wiped his forehead with his cardigan sleeve.

No reaction.

Some girl wanted a Virgin Mary. The waiter nodded and hurried off.

"For my next trick . . ." his voice trailed.

Do it right.

Do it right.

But I am! Why don't they see?

The MC whispered, "Half your time's gone."

Half? Corky wiped his forehead again. It was bad, no question so far there wasn't triumph in the wind, but that was his fault, and winning them back was up to him too and the best way to do that was go right for the throat, forget the order, he'd programmed wrong, the estimation was wrong, a bad idea, it took too goddam long for everybody to count their cards, a mistake, sure, but not irreconcilable, not if you do it right, and that had to be his bombshell number, the encore number, the one you lay it all out on, live or die with.

"The rising aces," Corky said.

It was as difficult a sleight as there was, involving a five lift —he'd never done a five lift in public before, never even for Merlin, just over and over in front of his mirror, because in a five lift you had to take the top five cards only you plucked them so it looked like one. Your fingers had to be so deft that you casually grabbed the top card but all the time you were hefting four more but if you slipped, if your hands were wet or shaky or in any way less than perfect, you blew it all.

He went back to the pretty girl he'd used first. He handed her a pack. "Would you take out the four aces please?"

It took a while.

Silence. Cloaking the room. But that was all right. It was build. There was a purpose to it. You had to make them think you were in trouble for the rising aces. You had to misdirect them, let them think you were scrambling so they didn't watch all that close.

"Now what?"

"Put them on top of the deck."

She did.

"All right now. The four aces are on the top of the deck next to each other, is that right?"

"Um-hmm."

"Now take a card from the bottom and cover the aces."

She put the bottom card on top of the aces.

Corky reached for the deck, held it out in full view. No quick moves, no moves at all, just kept the deck there. "All right. In this trick . . ." His voice trailed off again, this time intentionally. He tried to smile, "I did that wrong. You don't cover the aces yet, that's a different trick." He flicked off the top card.

With a five lift.

And he did it right. He had all five cards in one hand and he waved them a second, his wonderful hands moving so gracefully, as if it was really only one card, and then he casually shifted hands, and while he did, back palmed the four aces perfectly, stuck the top card into the middle of the deck. Then he returned the cards to the girl. "Okay, what have we got now? Four aces next to each other on top, right?"

"Umm-hmm."

"Okay. What I want you to do is make the aces rise."

"Me?" the pretty girl said.

"That's right. Just say, 'Aces rise.' "

"Aces rise."

Nothing happened.

"Hmmm," Corky said, "it doesn't seem to be working." Sweat was covering his face now. He could feel his shirt sticking tight to his skin.

A guy ordered a bourbon and branch water, no ice.

Corky paused until the waiter was gone. He had them now and he didn't want to blow his climax. Because the whole room *knew* the aces were on top of the deck in the girl's hands while all the time he had them back palmed in his own. "I can't figure why this trick isn't working," Corky said, sweat streaming down, "unless it might be because aces don't like cold weather and it's freezing in here. Brrr." And while he said "brrr" he reversed the back palm, started rubbing his hands together as if to get them warm. Only now the aces were between his hands.

"Brrrr," Corky said again, rubbing his hands harder, giving a quick flick with his thumb. "Brrrr, I'm just so cold."

And the aces started to rise.

"Oh look," Corky said, "here come the aces now. Look at them rise." He kept rubbing his hands together, feigning cold while the sweat poured down. "Two aces. Three aces. All four." Corky looked out at the audience.

They looked back at him.

Two girls wondered where the ladies' room was. A waiter pointed it out.

Corky just stood there. They should be applauding. That was his *encore* number. Not five guys *ever* in the world could do what he'd just done. WHY WEREN'T THEY CLAPPING?

"For my next . . ." Corky began. He stopped. "I'd like to do for you now . . ." He stopped. "This one . . . ummm . . . it's . . ." He stopped. And then suddenly it just burst out of him. "Jesus Christ," he said to the room, "do you know how *hard* that was? That's a thousand hours of my life you just watched."

The MC was beside him now. "Time's about up," he said. "Thanks."

"I did it right," Corky told him.

The MC nodded. "Swell."

Corky started off.

"What about your cards?" came the pretty girl's voice.

He stopped, shook his head, kept on going this time for the door. When he got outside he thought he'd probably go to pieces or something.

It didn't dawn on him for maybe half a block that he'd already gone . . .

Corky. The mirror. The cards. Ten fingers. Top card? Diamond four. He did a shift, controlled it to the center. Another shift, controlled it to the bottom. Diamond four on the bottom now. Now back to the top. His eyes. His eyes never left the mirror. The sleights were right. His eyes could not tell the moment the shifts came. It looked like magic. Now here, now there.

Corky. The mirror. The cards. The fingers like spiders now. He fanned the cards into a perfect semicircle. Snapped them together. He made the cards spring from one hand to the other, back and forth, the cards looked like an accordion.

Mistake #1: starting with the force on the pretty girl. Looked too easy. Should have started with a fan. Make the cards dance. Mistake #2: never do the estimations in public. People think it's a trick.

Corky. The mirror. The cards. The fingers moving on their own now. The mind moving too. Mistakes #3 to infinity: *CORKY WITHERS.* He was the only thing wrong. It didn't matter if he started with a flourish or a force, what mattered was he failed. He failed because Merlin said what magic was, magic was entertainment and he didn't entertain. Magic was winning the people and what had he won? Ever? All the years of his life, he had wanted most to please people and who had he ever pleased. So what did it matter if you started with a fan, the truth was the truth.

Nobody gave a shit.

Nobody had, did, or would.

Face that.

He shivered. How cold was it? He dialed weather. Not so cold. Why the shivering then? The mechanical voice said it might drop down on Wednesday. Corky hung up.

Corky. The mirror. The cards. The—Wednesday? The voice said Wednesday and that meant Wednesday was tomorrow and that was wrong, Tuesday was tomorrow, he had come straight from the Stardust and had sat by the mirror and so it had to be still Monday evening.

All the curtains and blinds were closed. Corky peered outside. Blinding. I must have sat the night through without knowing it. Weird.

Corky. The mirror. The—he called the mechanical voice again. Now it told him tomorrow was Thursday. Could that be? Another day gone. How long had he been sitting without sleep?

And how could he have shouted at the audience like that? What *difference* did it make the number of hours he'd practiced? That wasn't their problem. They were there to be entertained and *pleased.* And that he would never be able to do.

What time was it now? Probably he should eat something. He went to the icebox. The milk smelled. *What day was it?* How long had he been sitting at the mirror? He had to leave by Friday. He looked outside the window again. Night now. Thursday probably. A hundred hours without sleep? Smart. What a clever way to kill yourself. He'd have to be gone tomorrow. Out of the place tomorrow. All packed by tomorrow. Packed? What was there? Some cards and a mirror and forget it.

Corky. The cards. The fingers in the mirror. Look at the fingers. They never tired. A hundred hours they moved and watch them go. And who cared. Not him, not anymore. He didn't care about much of anything except he was bored with sticking around. Don't be an amateur anymore.

Do it right.

For once in your life do it right.

He turned off the lights and turned on the gas and lay on the couch, starting to drift. Comfortable. At last he was comfortable. And warm. No shivers anymore. He worried that the gas smell might be bad, but it wasn't, and as it grew stronger he grew used to it. His body was draining now. Emptying wonderfully. His eyelids flickered. That was fine. They deserved it. After a hundred hours, they had a right to close. His breathing was deep now. Deep and regular and fine.

". . . what is that stink . . ."

"Huh?"

". . . smells like gas . . ."

"It is gas." Corky blinked. "Who are you, how'd you get in here?"

". . . been here all the time . . . why are you killing yourself, it seems silly, killing yourself with your future . . ."

"What future—*who are you?*"

". . . that's not what Merlin said . . ."

"What did Merlin say?"

". . . he said you were better than Thurston at the same age . . ."

"No he didn't."

". . . and as good as Leipzig . . . he said if you kept at it, you were going to be as good as the game . . ."

Corky found himself weeping. "I just don't want to fail anymore, I'm tired."

". . . of course you're tired, you haven't slept for a hundred hours . . ."

"Did he really say as good as the game?"

". . . no . . ."

"I didn't think so."

". . . better . . . if you kept at it, you could leave them all behind . . ."

"I would like that."

". . . of course you would . . ."

"Merlin never lied. He must have meant it."

". . . you better get some rest . . . you have to be in perfect shape to leave them all behind . . ."

"Yes."

". . . sleep . . ."

"I will."

". . . turn off the gas first, why don't you . . ."

"All right."

". . . that's a good boy . . ."

"I hope I don't fail again. I don't know if I could take that."

". . . you can't fail . . . not anymore . . . I won't let you . . ."

"Promise?"

". . . promise . . ."

Corky got up, turned off the gas, lay back down on the couch again. He shook his head a little, kind of smiled. "Merlin used to think I was crazy. Sometimes I think he was right."

". . . no . . . you *were* crazy . . . you're fine now . . ."

THE POSTMAN

The line snaked down the block. The Postman moved along the sidewalk, idly counting. Forty-six. Forty-six people waiting for what maybe at the most could be a half dozen cancellations.

When you're hot, you're hot.

He glanced at his watch, saw it was nine, moved to the sidewalk in front of the Stardust because if nothing else, Goldstone was prompt.

At 9:02 the limo pulled up. He was kind of an aging boy wonder, Goldstone, thirty-eight now, but he'd been head of programming for CBS when he was thirty. NBC stole him, ABC tried like hell to crib him from the Sarnoffs, and the kicker on the whole thing, at least from the Postman's point of view, was that wherever he worked, when George Goldstone ran things, eventually your ratings went down.

But he had that survivor's instinct of knowing just *before* the Titanic would hit the iceberg, and moved on accordingly. He was your standard show business example of failing upwards, and the Postman had no doubts that eventually Goldstone would be running a major Hollywood film studio into receivership.

They shook hands perfunctorily and the Postman, who like many bald men knew more about wigs than beauticians, was struck again by the perfection of Goldstone's mop. Must have cost a thousand.

They started into the club. The Postman indicated the line, muttered "slow night tonight" and Goldstone answered nothing, just paused briefly and looked at the sign in the window that said, "Say Hello to Corky Withers" and below that, the standard smiling photo. "So that's your latest *wunderkind*," Goldstone said.

"Twenty-six record breaking weeks," he said modestly.

"Then how come I never heard of him?"

"You were so busy coming up with a sequel to *Beacon Hill* you probably missed a lot of things. Tampax got invented. The world rockets along, George."

They walked into the club. It looked even shabbier than usual. Goldstone cased it a moment. "High tone establishment you booked him into, Postman."

"I didn't book him, he was here. Likes it. I'm breaking my balls trying to budge him."

"I'm supposed to help with the budging, is that it?"

The Postman looked at the taller man seriously. "Nossir, you are not. You are in the talent business and I am not selling this kid to you or nobody. But when a blockbuster is about to explode, I don't want you running around screaming why didn't I give you a chance at him."

They were escorted to a table in the most distant corner. "I see they know you, ringside and everything."

"We can talk better here, we can see good enough."

"Blockbuster you said."

"Fucking skyrocket with luck. Never been a magician like him."

"Shit," George Goldstone said. "You dragged me down here for a *magician?*"

"Don't start, huh?"

"Magicians bomb on the tube—we can't book 'em into kiddie shows on Saturday anymore."

"Your father was an agent working for me, you little fart, don't tell me what bombs."

"That was before you got senile," Goldstone said.

"This kid—"

"—Ben, you're always trying to hustle magicians—you're a magic nut, terrific, don't inflict your neuroses on the rest of us."

"What's magic—don't answer, that was rhetorical—magic is misdirection. And misdirection is getting them to look in the wrong place at the right time. Well *of course* magic's had troubles with tv—you can't misdirect a goddam camera—ginger ale," he said to the waiter and looked at Goldstone.

"Scotch on the rocks. Pinch or Chivas."

"We got Clan MacGregor."

Goldstone looked at the Postman. "What am I *doing* here? With a lot of soda," he said to the waiter.

The club was full now.

The drinks came.

Goldstone sipped his Clan MacGregor. "I'll get you for this," he said to the Postman.

Now, on the stage, the bearded MC. "Say hello to Corky Withers," he said.

Goldstone watched as the magician in the gray cardigan and slacks walked onto the stage. There was considerable applause. Withers looked around nervously, nodded a few times. The applause quieted then, and he reached into his cardigan sweater.

"Ordinary cards," he began. "See?" He took one pack, pulled the cards out, handed them to a stunning girl at a ringside table. The girl looked at the cards, gave them back.

"He's not exactly loaded with stage presence," Goldstone whispered.

"He warms up as he goes along," the Postman answered. "And I think he knows you're here."

"I'd like you to pick one," Withers said to the stunning girl and she did. "Would you look at it please?" She did that too. "Is it the six of clubs?" She nodded. "Thank you," he said and took the card back.

Silence in the club. One or two people clapped once or twice.

Goldstone bent close to the Postman. "Dynamite opening," he whispered sarcastically. "Does he actually get better? Hard to believe."

The Postman just gave him a look.

"The rising aces," Withers said.

The Postman leaned close to Goldstone. "This trick is really incredible."

"Would you take out the aces please," he said to another girl at a ringside table, not as pretty as the first one, but with a better body. She fumbled through the deck, finally got the aces together. "Now put them on top of the deck and cover them with another card." She followed his instructions, handed the deck back. Then Withers said, "I'm sorry, my mistake, you don't cover the aces yet, that's a different trick," and he reached to take off the top card.

And someone shouted, "He's gonna do a five lift, *watch him, watch him*—"

Goldstone looked in the corner, tried to spot the heckler. "Fuckin' drunks," he said.

Withers ignored the interruption, took off the top card, started to go on. "All right, what we have here are the four aces on top of the deck and—"

"—bullshit," came from the corner. "They're in your left hand."

Withers blinked. He was beginning to perspire lightly now. "Um . . . yes, the aces—"

"—show us your left hand—that's right, show the hand not holding the deck, go on, go on—"

Withers glared into the corner. "I'm sorry," he said, "I'd appreciate it if you let me do what I get paid for."

"This isn't a charity ward?"

A few people started laughing now.

Withers was more flustered. "I'm not capable of working like this—if you know so much and you want to take over, by all means feel free."

The heckler said, "Don't wanna break my neck getting up there, give me a hand." Withers moved into the crowd.

And the crowd began applauding.

"What's going on?" Goldstone said.

No reply from the Postman.

Goldstone looked over in the corner where Withers and the heckler were. "You really think you know a lot, don't you?" Withers said to the heckler as he moved back onto the stage.

Goldstone smiled. "Cute idea," he said to the Postman. "The heckler being a dummy."

"I'll guaranfuckingtee ya I'm an expert," the dummy said.

"What's the dummy's name?" Goldstone wondered.

"Fats is what Corky calls him," the Postman said.

"Well you ruined the rising aces," Corky said, standing there, holding Fats in one arm.

Fats leaned close and started whispering. "Do you see that beautiful girl, the one you did the trick with?"

"What about her?"

"I think she likes me."

"Don't be ridiculous."

"I wonder if she does—maybe she'd enjoy a little roll in the shavings with me."

"I don't think you're funny," Corky said.

"Well *they* do," Fats said, pointing to the audience, who were laughing. "Women go for me in a big way—I can do everything except get a soft-on. I suppose if I really needed one, I could always borrow yours."

"I don't want to talk about my sex life," Corky said.

"Tell us all about it, we've got half a minute to waste."

The audience laughed louder. "Don't encourage him," Corky told them.

Goldstone watched as the audience began applauding. "Is that a punch line of his?"

The Postman nodded.

"I'd like to do something for you now," Corky told the people. "Even I don't know how or why it works, but for some strange reason, if I take a diamond and hold it long enough, it turns into a heart." He turned to Fats, and held out a deck. "Choose any diamond."

Fats clutched a diamond six.

"Show the people."

Corky helped him raise his arm.

"Now if you'll give it back I'll just—"

"—give it back my ass. If you're a real magician, change it while I'm holding it."

"Moving on," Corky said, "I would now like to—"

"—you mean you're not gonna make it change?"

"Not with you holding it, obviously. You're really impossible tonight, I'd like to change the subject until you simmer down." Corky stopped, pointed out toward the Postman. "Ladies and gentlemen, a man who means a great deal to me is here this evening, say hello please to my agent, Mr. Ben Greene, the Postman. Stand up, would you Ben?"

The Postman stood and everybody looked and applauded.

"Keep standing—please—I'd like to say a few things about what you mean to me and Fats."

"He's a great agent," Fats said. "Corky and I feel honored because mostly, the Postman handles the biggies: Dick Contino—he's the fella told Mario Lanza to go on a diet—it's thanks to the Postman that right now in Stratford Tab Hunter is playing Gertrude—that's a coup, folks—and he's not just interested in show biz, nossir, he knows his politics too—handles Wilbur Mills' presidential campaign, don't you?—and here's the climax folks—and remember you heard it here first: tonight the Postman has concluded an exhausting session of negotiations climaxing in the following announcement: Miss Vicki has just been booked into the Superdome. Thanks, Ben, you can sit down now."

The Postman sat down and glanced across the table. "Sorry you came?"

Goldstone drank his Scotch. "Kid's good," he said.

"That was nothing—I got maybe the best magician in fifty years matched with the first X rated dummy on the block. Eat your heart out."

"I'd like to do some estimations now," Corky said.

"Hey wait—" Fats said. "I got this six of diamonds, you said you'd change it to a heart."

"You ruined that too," Corky said.

"Omigod," Fats said then. "Look—" Corky helped him raise his arm. "It turned into a heart while I was holding it." He looked at Corky, shook his head.

"How'd he *doooo* that?" Fats called loudly, and the audience applauded again.

"How *did* he do it?" Goldstone asked the Postman. That was before he ordered a double Clan MacGregor.

The Postman just sat back and smiled . . .

*   *   *

On the way to the dressing room between shows, the Post-man said, "It's a funny thing, but he bombed here bad on an amateur night."

"Hard to believe."

"Well he didn't have the dummy then. He disappeared about a year, came back again with Fats, and they booked him regular. The rest, as they say, is gonna be history. I don't think he's hit twenty-eight yet." He knocked. "Me," the Post-man said.

From inside Fats said, "Oh shit, it's gangrene."

Goldstone laughed. "Gangrene—that's funny."

They walked in. "Just wanted to make an introduction, Corky. This is George Goldstone."

Corky got up. "How do you do, sir." He held Fats in one arm.

"Nice act," Goldstone said. "Lot of potential."

"Wouldn't it be nice if you were right," Corky said.

"What about me?" Fats said.

"Behave, huh?" Corky said.

Goldstone smiled. "Lot of funny stuff, Fats."

"Thank you, Mr. Wigstone." Fats was staring at Goldstone's hairpiece.

"That's what *I* call funny," the Postman said.

Fats leaned close to Corky. "Is this the same George Gold-stone that's so famous in the tv trade? The one known as 'Limp Dick George'?"

"He doesn't mean anything," Corky said.

The Postman was roaring.

"You'll strain your pacemaker," Fats said. He turned to Goldstone. "I don't know why he's laughing, he hasn't had an erection since Coolidge was president."

Goldstone began to go on that.

"I apologize," Corky said. "He's been impossible all day."

"You're a very talented young man."

Corky smiled.

"Is it true you've never missed a show of Captain Kangaroo?" Fats asked Goldstone.

"On that," Goldstone said, and he waved and started outside. "Can I ask one thing? How *did* you change the diamond to the heart?"

"I'm the misdirection," Fats said. "While we're bullshitting around, he could bring an elephant onstage."

"Which is why," the Postman said, "*this* magician wouldn't be anything but sensational on the tube. The camera watches their faces, not Corky's hands." He looked at Goldstone. "Be with you in a sec'."

Goldstone nodded, left.

The Postman shut the door.

"It went okay?" Corky asked.

"Calling Mr. Goldstone 'Limp Dick George' may not have advanced our cause, but on the whole I would say, if I play him smart and don't get pushy, it was incanfuckingdescent." He looked at Fats. "See? You're catching."

"What happens now?" Corky wondered.

"Nothing very dramatic. A lounge in Vegas for a little. I can get you on the Shore and the Walters and the Griffin. Eventually you'll shift headquarters to New York, better media exposure there. You'll come back out here, do a couple Carsons, and how's that for openers, enough?"

Corky nodded.

"You're a good kid, Corky."

"The dummy is the talent," Fats said.

The Postman left them then.

Silence.

Then whispering: "Corky?"

"Hmm?"

"Remember the night we first teamed up? When you did that dumb thing with the gas? Remember what I promised?"

Corky nodded. "No more failure."

"Do you believe me now?"

Nod.

"Corky?"

"What?"
"You know what I think?"
"What do you think?"
"We're gonna be a star . . ."

3. THE WORK IS DONE

1

"How much farther do you think to Grossinger's?" Corky asked.

"Dunno," the cabdriver said. He was a kid, quick-eyed, always with a cigarette in the left corner of his mouth. He slurred when he spoke. "We'd a been there now if you hadn't said 'take the shortcut.'"

"Sorry," Corky answered. "I thought I knew this area better than I do, I guess. Been over fifteen years since I've seen it."

"We'll get there," the driver said.

Corky nodded. The sun was starting to drop rapidly now—in half an hour it would be dark. The quiet road curved downhill through the remains of a multicolored forest. The turning of the leaves was just about over. The Catskills were still pretty, but age was coming fast.

There were two suitcases on the seat beside him. Corky opened the fat bag and reached in for a deck of cards. He sat back then, did a one hand shuffle. It was extraordinarily difficult to execute under ideal conditions, but riding fast in a badly sprung car didn't help. The first time he tried it he got through it, but not neatly. He tried it again: holding the deck in one hand, with that hand alone dividing the deck in half; then the hardest part, forcing the cards through each other, an ordinary riffling motion, simplicity with both hands, with one alone God knows how many hours of practice.

Corky shifted the cards, did the stunt again, with his left hand this time. For no reason he could ever fathom, he always did this better with the left hand than the right. Corky watched his fingers dancing. What a dumb thing to be able to do—it was of no value in close-up work; there were no tricks that depended for completion on being able to shuffle a deck of cards quickly and efficiently with but one hand. Sometimes it held its weight as a kind of flourish, to show dexterity, but all in all, it was pointless. There were probably six around anywhere who could do it with either hand: the two Japs, the Frenchman, maybe two more here in the States. Corky wondered for a moment if they ever watched their hands and reflected on the waste involved. How many times had their fingers cramped trying to get the riffle right? Merlin was always after him to give it up, quit throwing away the days.

What else did he have to do with them back then?

"Stop here!" Corky said suddenly.

"Huh?" from the driver.

There had been a quick flash of blue water to the left. "Just slow down will be fine."

The car slowed.

Corky rolled down the window and stared out at the water. "I think that's Lake Melody."

"If you say so."

"Looks just the same." He continued to stare. "No it doesn't, it looks a lot smaller; it's nothing really and I would have sworn it was huge."

"You want me to stay slow?"

"There should be some cabins up around the curve."

There were. Set down in the woods, a good distance off the road. A larger main house and then, below it, maybe two dozen white cabins around the lake. A bungalow colony. They passed a flaking sign: FINAST BUNGALOWS. And below that, in smaller lettering: ALONE ON THE SHORES OF LAKE MELODY.

"Now stop," Corky said, and this time, the car did.

The driver looked out. "Must have been pretty."

"Oh yes," Corky answered, getting out, quickly walking across the road, staring down at the empty-looking buildings below in the woods. "I won't be a sec'," he called to the driver, and with that, he put his hands in his pockets and started down toward the main house. The ground was covered with leaves, and his steps made the only sound. It was colder up here than it had been back in the city, and he shivered suddenly. He was wearing just a cotton shirt and his blazer and his shaking began to grow. He slapped his arms across his body, rubbed his hands across his chest, broke into a half run, getting the circulation going.

He was still cold.

"Anybody?" he called as he reached the main house. "Hey?"

"What do you want?" from indoors. Female voice; distant.

"Cabin?"

"We're kind of closed."

Above him now, behind screens and glass on the second floor, a face was vaguely visible. "Something near the lake is really what I'm after. Close as you've got."

"We're not really set up for guests just now."

"This is just the kind of place I'm looking for is the thing. I won't be disturbed here."

"That's for sure."

"Pay you for a week, I won't stay near that long."

From behind the window now, hesitation. "I've got no services to offer."

"Pay you fifty bucks a night, how's that?"

"I'm not turning down fifty bucks."

"Lemme get my stuff," Corky said, and he spun, started back up the long hill toward the road. He jogged easily, conscious of his breathing, the little bursts of white hitting the air as he exhaled. It was getting colder fast, but he wasn't shivering anymore.

The cabdriver was standing by his car, smoking. "All set?"

"Little change in plan," Corky told him.

The driver looked at Corky.

Corky looked back, then quickly away, because he had caught the guy studying him a couple of times in the rearview mirror, and usually what that meant, nowadays, was that they recognized him from somewhere. Corky got his two bags out of the back. "What do I owe you?"

The driver sat behind the wheel, glanced at the meter. "Exactly eighty-eight dollars and ninety-five cents, as you can see for yourself."

Corky reached for his wallet. He had gone to the bank just before leaving town, and he took out some bills. Now he glanced at the driver again. Corky hesitated. "What'll make you happy?" he said finally.

"Let your conscience be your guide. I might get lost on the way back, have car trouble, all kinds of things, but don't let that enter into your thinking."

"Here's a hundred," Corky said, handing over one bill.

The driver took it, said a very quiet, "Thanks."

"You don't understand," Corky told him. "That's just for you. This"—and he brought out the second hundred—"this should cover the meter with enough for maybe a cup of coffee thrown in."

"Hey you're my man," the driver said.

"You're welcome," Corky said; "I like the way you handle a car. Plus one more thing."

"What's 'at?"

"You didn't bring me here."

The driver looked up at him.

"Am I still your man?"

The driver nodded.

"Keep it that way." Corky picked up his luggage, smiled. "Take it easy."

"Any way I can get it," the driver said, starting the car, waving, gunning off, gone.

Corky turned and headed back down the hill toward the main house where the woman he had spoken to before was waiting. She wore a blue sweater over gray slacks, blue sneakers. "You said near the water, didn't you?"

"That should be the quietest, don't you think?"

"They're none of them exactly noisy just now."

"Well the prettiest anyway."

She nodded, started leading him down away from the main house through the woods toward the water. The sun was almost gone now, and the remains of it rebounded off the lake into their eyes. Corky walked quietly behind her, carrying his cases. "I'll give you the best we got," she said, as they approached the farthest cabin, set very close to the water, a good hundred yards from the main house.

"I have the money ready," Corky said.

"Don't you want to see it first?"

"I'm sure it'll be fine."

She got out a key, shook her head. "What a weird thing, keeping everything locked up—not a whole lot to steal."

Corky nodded.

She opened the door, stepped inside. He followed. "Nothing all that special. Living room here, bedroom in there"—she pointed. "Bedroom's small but the bed's good." Now she pointed again. "And the fireplace works. You got a view of the lake out this way, you can look up into the woods across there."

"It's fine," Corky said. "Let me pay you now." He put down his bags.

"Bathroom in there—kitchenette behind the curtain there. That's it."

"Like I said," Corky told her. "Fine." He held out two fifties. "One for tonight and one in advance. If I stay tomorrow, we'll talk finances then, okay?"

"Whatever." She folded the money, rolled it again, held it tight in her hand. "If you need—" and she stopped.

"Go on."

"I was gonna say 'if you need anything, call' but there's nothing up at the main place. When I said we were closed, I wasn't whistling Dixie." She started toward the door. "Probably I should have said, 'if you need anything, don't call.'" She gave a little wave. "'Bye."

Corky nodded.

The second she closed the door Fats was saying, "Open up, open up," in a muffled tone from the larger suitcase.

"Shhhh—"

"—don't you 'shhh' me, schmucko, just open the goddam lid or there's gonna be major league trouble."

Corky got Fats out, then went to the window away from the lake and watched as the girl walked up toward the main house.

"I hate the country already," Fats said. "It's quiet and full of leaves. All you hear when you walk around is crunch crunch crunch."

Corky said nothing.

The sunlight hit the girl's long dark blonde hair.

"I thought we were going to Grossinger's. At least Grossinger's got action. This dump here, maybe it'd do for a coroners' convention, but otherwise, forget it."

Corky still was silent, still watched.

"Hey, why the silent act, what's up?"

Corky shook his head. "She never once remembered me."

"Who? The broad? How can you blame her, she's verging on the gorgeous and you are a pretty forgettable fella. No. Take that back—actually, your pointy head is quite distinctive, I wouldn't think anybody could forget that. Must have been your acne clearing up that made her not know you."

"You're not funny! Not even a goddam little."

"Sounds like I stepped on a corn—how come I'm not funny?"

Corky's voice got soft. "'Cause that was Peggy Ann Snow."

2

She walked into the house and locked the door, which she always did when she was alone around the place. Then she went to the tv, flicked it on, which she also always did whenever it got dark, whether she was alone around the place or not.

News.

She looked at it vacantly for a moment; the local news guy was as intelligent as ever but she had difficulty focusing her attention on what he was saying. Financial stuff. Cities going bust.

Maybe some music.

Off with the tv, on with the radio. She listened. Elton John? It was hard for her now to tell them from each other. She had a bunch of cousins who were like twelve, and they always hooted when she said it was all the same, every one of them, boom, boom, boom with the rhythm section, that's all there was. No words anymore, why shouldn't they sound the same. But then her folks had been like that, unable to distinguish Anka from Rydell from Fabian when she'd been a kid and they were old.

Only I'm not old.

Elvis!

Off went the radio and now, for the first time since she'd entered the house, she picked up the pace a little. She knelt quickly by the record shelf underneath the hi-fi, took out the first Presley she happened to hit. It was his "Golden Records" and Peg looked at his face on the front for a while, then turned the record over and studied the listings:

Hound Dog
Teddy Bear

> Love Me Tender
> Don't Be Cruel

Those were *songs*. Peg turned on the machine, took out the record, reached for her special cloth and went over the disc carefully before she put it on the spindle. All her Elvis recordings were in perfect shape and that was not about to change. Now she pushed the start lever, waited . . .

> 'Since my baby left me'—WHAP—
> 'Found a new place to dwell'—WHAP—
> 'Down at the end of lonely street
> At Heartbreak Hotel . . .'*

She knew exactly who she was and where she was when that first Presley hit home. Sneaking a cigarette in Viola Schenker's car. Closing in on thirteen. Body already formed. She'd listened then and could not believe—there was no way she could hear what she was hearing. Never mind what the sentences said, what the singer was saying was "Let's screw—*you* I'm talking to, don't look away. *Now!*"

Not in the mood for Elvis either. She lifted the tone arm off, and in the ensuing silence, put the record back in the sleeve, then into the envelope, then back to the shelf.

Eat something?

Not hungry.

She got out her high school graduation yearbook. Turned to the full-page picture. It was the front of the sports section, and there she was, caught at the peak of her jump, arms out, legs spread, smiling. The caption said simply: "Peggy Snow scores one for our side."

She looked at the picture awhile. Of course the cheerleader's costume was ridiculous, but otherwise . . .

She carried the book to a mirror, lifted up the photo, put it beside her face. Studied them. She looked fine. Fine.

But her depression only deepened.

She walked to the kitchen, opened some cat food, put it in

* "Heartbreak Hotel" © 1956 by Tree Publishing Co., Inc.

Sherlock's bowl. Then she opened the back door, knocked the dish against the knob, called his name. He was waiting and inside in no time. She put the dish down. Sherlock ate. He was a large, powerful and totally individualistic beast and he never allowed her to hold him except when he was done eating.

She picked Sherlock up then, walked to the window, stared down toward the lake and the one lit cabin.

"He didn't remember me," Peg said . . .

3

Corky scuffed his way along the shore of Lake Melody. In Chicago it might get dignified with the word "pond." Not more than a mile around probably. But up here, anything you could get your body into was Lake something. This one wasn't even all that pretty—the land surrounding, yes, lovely, but the water itself had a mud bottom and even on the nicest days, you always were on the lookout for snapping turtles. No one had even seen one around, but you just knew that if you were a snapper, Lake Melody was the kind of place you'd like to call home.

He glanced up toward the main house. The lights glowed out, a bright barrier against the surrounding darkness. Corky stopped and turned, taking in the whole place. A little light from his cabin; the others, nothing but shapes. Dead beasts.

When he was a kid, the Catskills had millions of these places: bungalow colonies. Mom and Pop operations. Often they made the cabins themselves or hired the local carpenter, usually drunk. And they survived by their summer rentals. All the people who couldn't afford the big places would come, and book a cabin for the summer, and let the kids run while the mothers sat in chairs, rocking and gossiping till the weekends when the breadwinners arrived. You did your own cooking, cleaned for yourselves. What you rented was the roof mainly. Usually a game room in the main house where the Mom and Pop ruled.

Only now, at least from the way things looked on the drive up, it was hard times in the Catskills. Sure, Grossinger's was probably minting money and The Concord was still trying to convince the masses that they'd stumbled into Vegas, but the smaller places, the colonies, good-bye and amen.

Sad.

Corky started walking faster, heading for his cabin. When he got there, he unlocked the door, went inside, started to undress. He had his pants half off when he glanced into the bathroom, saw there wasn't any soap or towels. He slipped his trousers back on, rebuttoned his shirt, reached for his blazer. After that he grabbed Fats and took off. There wasn't much moon, but enough to make out a kind of worn route that led toward the main house. Corky hurried, stumbling once or twice over tree roots, but never enough to make him come close to falling. There was no sound coming from the main house and his knock echoed. "I'm sorry," Corky said loudly.

From above, on the second floor: "What do you want?"

"No soap."

"I told you you wouldn't like it; you leaving already?"

Corky started laughing. "I didn't mean 'no soap' that way—I meant there wasn't any. Or towels either."

"We never really supplied that stuff."

"Oh."

"Hold on a sec'. I'll get you something."

He waited on the steps listening to her footsteps inside. She was coming down the stairs. Then, the door was opening. "C'mon in—no sense waiting outside—"

"Thank you," Corky began, and as he took a few steps inside, he was prepared to say a good deal more, to apologize for being a bother, to—

"—omigod, you brought Fats along," Peg cried with excitement.

Corky just stood there.

"And you thought Peg didn't remember," Fats said.

She looked at Corky. "You knew who I was too?"

Corky made a nod.

"Why didn't you two at least grunt at each other or something?" Fats wanted to know.

"I don't—I'm not really sure," Corky stammered—"See, she was upstairs and I couldn't really tell at first—there was the screen and the sun reflected off the glass—by the time I thought I knew, I figured she didn't know who I was or she would have said something."

"What's your story?" Fats asked.

"It's been so long," Peg said; "and I watch every chance I get—I see a lot of television so I don't think I've missed you once—I didn't want to embarrass anybody in case . . ."

Fats shook his head. "We're all so goddam sensitive I could whoopse."

Peg started laughing. "He's just as cute as on the tube."

"Cute!" Fats said loudly. "Virile, yes; sexy, absolutely. 'Cute' is for Disney, if you don't mind."

"I'm really excited," Peg said. "C'mon, c'mon," and she closed the door. Then she looked at Corky for a moment. Neither of them said anything.

"The little old matchmaker—me," Fats cut through.

Laughter.

Then: "Oh, can I hold him? Would that be all right?"

Corky hesitated.

"The answer is 'lemme at her,'" Fats said.

"Be kind of careful," Corky said.

"Promise." Peg took Fats with both hands. "He's heavy," she said, surprised.

"*Husky*, you thoughtless creature," Fats said.

Peg looked at Corky. "His lips didn't move."

"That's because you didn't work my levers, baby."

"What levers?" Peg asked.

Corky took Fats, laid him face down on a tabletop. "All a ventriloquist's doll really is, is a large wooden head, heavy like you said, with a wooden pipe leading down where the neck should be. There are levers on the pipe and when you work them, the dummy seems to come to life. At least, that's the theory." He pointed to Fats' overalls, slit up the back. "All dolls are slit like that—so you can get your hand in to the levers. The rest of the body is mainly strong canvas bindings and stuffing." He lifted Fats back into her arms. "Now try. Sit in a chair; might be better. Fats has extra levers, 'cause I've fixed him so he can smoke and cry, but don't bother with those."

Peg sat, took Fats, reached into the slit.

Fats began groaning sexually.

Peg broke out laughing.

"Don't mind him," Corky said.

"Let me look at you," Fats said.

"How do I do that?" Peg asked.

"That same pipe where the levers are—just turn it. See?"

Peg turned Fats' head till their eyes met. "This is kind of fun."

"Come wiz mee to zee Kazz-bah," Fats said.

"I still can't get his lips going."

"Up a little," Corky said.

She touched the right lever and Fats' lips went up and down.

"You don't know what life's like till you've had your levers fondled by a beautiful girl. Hit the lever just up from your hand," Fats told her.

She followed his instructions. His right eye winked at her.

Peg hugged Fats, both arms around him tight. Then she carefully took him, handed him back to Corky. "I really did enjoy that," she said.

Corky took Fats, said, "Anytime."

"Whisper," Fats said. Corky brought him up close to his ear. "She's very nice."

"Thank you, Fats," Peg said. She stood. "How do you *do* that? It's really like he's talking."

"Illusion mostly. I just turn my head and look at him when he shoots off his mouth, he does the same for me. You follow our eyes. Just illusion and practice is all."

"But your lips don't move."

"Neither do yours. Seriously. Open your mouth about a quarter inch and keep your lips still and try saying 'Hi Corky.'"

"Hi Corky."

"See how easy? Now try 'Bye Corky.'"

"'Bye Corky,'" Peg said. Then: "My lips moved that time."

"I know. On the 'B.' 'B' and 'P' and 'M' and 'W'—they are the toughies. Give six months or so to each letter and you'll be able to say 'beep' without moving your lips, big deal."

"'Wham' is also very hard," Fats said. "I went crazy till he got those right. 'Wham-beep-wham-beep.' If you're an intellectual sex pervert like me, that can get kind of monotonous. 'Pervert' is also hard. Usually Corky chickens out and says 'deviate.'"

"You should record all this," Peg told him, starting upstairs. "I really mean it."

"That's an interesting idea, thanks."

"Make a fortune, selling it to insomniacs," Fats said. He started intoning like a speech teacher. "The pebbles were moping because—"

"—enough outta you," Corky said.

Peg gestured for them to follow. "Come get what you need." They were all moving up when the scream came. Corky stopped. Peg continued on.

Again, from outside, the high pitched scream.

Peg looked down, smiled. "That's just my big old cat," she said. "Probably found a dead bird."

"Probably *made* a dead bird," Fats said.

"Sherlock isn't any too friendly. I call him Sherlock because he's always nosing into things. Loves poking around." She led them along the second floor corridor, opened the large closet at the end. "Help yourself."

Corky handed her Fats, moved into the large closet. Most of its contents were in closed cardboard boxes. Corky pointed to them. "Shutting up for the winter?"

"Permanent. Trying to get it ready to sell. Not that there's any mad rush on to buy the place. But the hope is that someone'll think the property's valuable, what with the lake and all."

"Folks still around?"

"Till a couple of seasons ago—now they've got kind of a one bedroom condo near Lauderdale in Florida—I tried keeping the place going, gave it my best shot, but the winters are too hard to cut anymore."

Corky took down some towels, several cakes of soap, an

extra blanket. "You used to have students during the winter."

"Sure. Married ones from that little college over the way. They closed it up this fall. That's closed, we're closed, most places like us are closed. Pretty soon I think they'll paint a big sign in the sky: 'Hey, everybody, the Catskills are closed.'"

Corky took Fats back, started down the stairs. "And what'll you do then?"

Peg shrugged. "Whatever."

Corky descended through the ensuing silence. He moved slowly down, then turned at the bottom, nodded thanks, turned, headed for the front door. He had his hand almost to the knob when Peggy said, "Hey you wouldn't want any coffee or anything?"

"Thank God," Fats replied. "I was just about to invite you to ask us."

"I'd like that a lot," Corky told her.

"Have you even eaten supper?"

Corky shook his head.

"I just know I've got a bottle of wine around someplace."

"Terrific," Corky said. "Let me just get my stuff down to the cabin and—"

"—*stuff?*" Fats said. "What *stuff* are you talking about? There's mostly *me* and I want to stay."

"Quick shower and I'll be up."

"I'll be in the kitchen slaving." She waved.

He returned it, then headed on out the door. He looked around, hesitated till he found the path, then hurried on down toward his cabin.

"She hugged me," Fats said.

"I saw."

"I suspect she found me irresistible."

"Don't we all."

"I wonder why she isn't married?"

"How do you know she isn't married?"

"Because, schmucko, if you weren't so unobservant you'd have noticed she didn't have no ring on."

Corky shrugged. He continued on in the moonlight until Fats screamed *"Christ!"* as the giant cat leaped out onto the path, the bloody remains of a headless bird in her mouth.

"Say hello to Sherlock," Corky said.

The cat dropped the bird and was gone.

"Look at that—Jesus."

"I think we were just made a peace offering." Corky slowed, studying the carcass. "Sparrow?"

"Who cares, let's go, let's go." Corky stepped over the bird and picked up his pace till he got to the cabin. Then he put Fats in the overstuffed chair, showered. Quickly, he dried himself, put on a different shirt, took his time combing his hair. Then he casually tossed his jacket over one shoulder, headed for the door.

"Question." from Fats.

Corky waited.

"How come we came here? I don't mean the Catskills, I mean this particular hot spot, Caesar's Palace transplanted to the shores of Lake Melody."

Corky shrugged. "No reason. Impulse. Luck. Fluke."

"Good," Fats said. "Then there's really no reason for our sticking around long."

"'Course not."

"Make damn sure you lock that door, huh?"

"Why?"

"Because, schmucko, I don't want that beast getting its claws into me."

Corky got the key. "Whatever you want." He started for the door again.

This time Fats said, "How long you gonna be?"

Corky shrugged. "Depends."

"You could be a little more specific."

"I don't think late."

"That's also good."

"Why?" Corky asked.

"If you were late, old Fats might start getting jealous . . ."

Long beat.

". . . and we wouldn't want that."

A longer one.

". . . would we now . . ."

4

"You never really told why you were here."

Corky answered, "The truth, I guess, is I'm hiding."

She looked at him. They were finishing dinner in the living room where she'd set up a card table by the fire. At first, it had been too hot, but as the meal went on, the fire softened, and they kept moving closer and closer, table, wine bucket, folding chairs. "From?"

"I just have to get my head on straight about a few things."

She nodded, took out the wine bottle. "I don't think you're supposed to chill it when it's red, but I figured the bucket added the proper note of elegance. When you entertain a lot, you learn little touches can really add up." She started to pour. "I was being funny," she said. "About my entertaining."

"It's very good wine."

"Gallo Hearty Burgundy. Won lots of blind tastings against those higher-priced French imports."

"I'm not really into wine much."

"When you run a fancy resort, you have to keep track of the trends," Peg told him. "Your head seems on pretty straight to me."

"I've been acting weird, believe me."

"If you say so."

"See I *thought* I was having an argument with my agent about a matter of principle. But earlier today, I was walking around the lake and I realized I'd been b.s.ing myself. It's the future's really got me scared. See, I guess I've got an outside chance at making it big, and I'm not sure I want to take it."

"I guess you are a little weird."

"Nobody's arguing with you about that. But there's a lot of hassling that goes along with success."

She nodded. "Should we eat at Sardi's or '21'? Should we hit the opera or the dance? Should I switch to Halston or stay faithful to Balenciaga? Could be murder."

"I'm a private person," Corky said.

"And if you make it, you think they'll find out all your secrets?"

Corky smiled.

"More?" She pointed to their plates.

"Thanks, I'm stuffed, it was delicious."

"I don't like to sound conceited, but anything Swanson freezes, I can thaw. For dessert there's Miss Lee's brownies or Mrs. Smith's pie." She smiled. "Years ago, Ronnie told me, 'Whenever possible, Birdseye.'" She stood up, reached for the plates. She was wearing a white satin blouse now, unbuttoned at the throat, and just the start of her breasts was occasionally visible in the firelight.

"Maybe dessert later, if that's okay."

"Whatever." She took their plates and started for the kitchen, concentrating on being careful not to spill, so Corky's "you're really beautiful," took her by surprise. "I'm not," she said before she said, "I only wish I was," followed by "but" and then she turned. "You think so?" She shook her head, remembering. "Hey that's right, I was always pretty for you."

"I didn't say you were pretty."

"Whatever." She finished her trip to the kitchen and called, "You didn't pick up on Ronnie."

"Is he important?"

"Mate. Consort. Spouse. I'm very big on enlarging my vocabulary."

"Are you very big on Ronnie?"

She came back. "How come you ask?"

He pointed to her hand. "No ring."

"We're separated as of this moment. We separate about every moon phase. It hasn't been your everyday Debbie Reynolds romance."

"Where is he now?"

Peg shrugged. "Humping some local beauty, I expect. I don't know where he is, but he'll be back tonight or a week from tonight or in between or after." She stopped by the couch. "You even remember who I'm talking about? Ronnie? 'Duke'?"

"I always figured you'd marry him."

"Why?"

"I don't know, just did, does he still look like Elvis Presley?"

The question sideswiped her. She managed an "Ohmi—" before she sank to the sofa, put her head to the cushions and wept.

Corky hurried over, sat down, reached out, almost touched her dark blonde hair, got up, hurried back to the table, brought her wineglass over. "Here," he said. "Hearty Burgundy. Very medicinal."

She continued to cry.

Corky sat there beside her. Again he reached out for her hair.

> . . . Peggy Ann Snow
> Peggy Ann—

He brought his hand back, made it go to his lap, kept it there.

Peg got up, kept her head turned away as she ran to the bathroom, closed the door. When she came out a few minutes later, she'd washed her face hard, scrubbed it, all makeup gone. "Admit it," she said, "*now* I'm beautiful."

"Little moist maybe."

She sat down again, began talking like Emily Post. "'Whenever the party shows signs of winding down, a quick burst of hysteria from the hostess is a sure way to get things giddy again.'" She looked at Corky. "Hey I'm sorry."

"You don't remember high school much I guess."

She shook her head. "Never think of those days."

"Not the cheerleading or anything; all the boys?"

"It's like it could have happened to somebody else."

"Thank God I didn't mention Pat Boone, you'd have really come unglued."

Peg thought that was funny. "You wanna know something crazy?" she asked after she was done laughing. "You're different when you're not working."

"What do you mean?"

"Doing your act. Like before with Fats. You *are* different when he's not around and that's the truth."

"You're very perceptive—you want to know something big league crazy, it's this: Fats does most of his own lines."

"I don't get that."

"It's like an acting exercise: 'make believe you're a tree.' Only *I* make believe I'm Fats. I do it all the time. Not on the bus or in Grand Central Station—people might run for a straitjacket. But when I'm rehearsing, if I get stuck for a joke or an insult, I just call on old Fats."

"And it works?"

"He's been infuckingfallible most of the time," Corky said, doing Fats.

"I wish I was talented," Peg said.

"I don't know if I'm so talented," Corky told her. "I think I'm a little flaky if you want to know the truth."

Peg stood up and smiled. "You always used to do that."

"What?"

"Put yourself down. Why do you think that is?"

Corky shrugged, watched her empty the wine bottle into her glass. "We'll split this last, okay? No—tell you what—I'll send the *sommelier*—pretty impressive, huh?—I think I've got another Gallo job, it hasn't been breathing but let's open it and live."

Corky didn't know what to say.

"I'm not trying to get you drunk, don't worry."

Corky smiled. "I really oughtta be getting back."

"You have to take the sitter home, is that it?"

"It's been kind of a wild day; I'm beat."

"Sure?"

Corky stood, stretched. "I ought to get back."

"Fats doesn't like being alone?"

Corky laughed. "Ya got me."

She walked him to the door, kissed him. Quickly. Up on tip-toe, lips to cheek, no big deal.

Still, Corky didn't mind it a bit. He waited outside a moment after she closed the door, almost knocked, turned, hurried back to the cabin and had the door half unlocked when Fats asked, "How was the orgy?" from the overstuffed chair.

"Oh stop it." Corky closed the door behind him.

"What was it, a fifty course meal? You sure didn't break your ass getting back here."

"I could have stayed longer!"

"Ohh-hoo-hoo—stepped on a corn again."

Corky started getting undressed.

"She got the hots for you?"

"You will be thrilled to learn that the high point of the evening was when I reduced her to tears."

"Hey schmucko, attaway."

Corky finished undressing, went into the bathroom.

Distant: "Hey, when are we bugging out of here?"

Corky said, "I don't know, haven't given it all that much thought. Tomorrow, the day after."

"Well I'm a city boy, the sooner the quicker."

Corky closed the door, closed his eyes.

> . . . Peggy Ann Snow
> Peggy Ann Snow
> Please let me fol—

Muffled: "Hey, what'd you close the door for?"

"I'm pissing, do you mind?"

"Ooh-hoo-hoo; dainty, ain't he?"

Corky peed, washed, brushed his teeth. He walked back into the bedroom, turned off the lights, got into bed, lay there.

"That's it, huh?—no recap of the evening?"

"Nothing happened—no—not totally true—she pecked me on the cheek when I left."

"Was it a French peck? Were her lips open?"

Corky laughed. "A French peck is a funny idea."

"Just don't you ever forget who the real talent is."

Corky rolled over and faced the wall.

"'Night," from Fats.

Corky grunted, shut his eyes.

> . . . Peggy—

"—are you thinking of her?"

"What?"

"The truth."

"Oh, Jesus."

"You *were*."

"Bullshit."

"And in the bathroom too—that's why you closed the door—"

"—for chrissakes *stop!*"

Pause. Then, softer: "You're not lying?"

"I don't. Not to you. Have I ever?"

Long pause. "I sound like a fucking fishwife, don't I?"

"You said it, I didn't."

"I don't know what's with me today."

"It's all this fresh air most likely."

"Sleep well, Laddie. And I'm sorry."

Corky tried a snore. Another.

Nothing from Fats.

> . . . Peggy Ann Snow . . .
> . . . Peggy Ann Snow . . .
> Please-*Please-Please!* . . .

5

Peg happened to be looking at her watch at the time, so she knew it was precisely at 3:35 the following afternoon that Corky began to behave, for want of a better word, crazy.

"Began" wasn't really it. His behavior had been growing erratic for a while earlier, only she had chosen not to pay attention.

Mistake.

But the day had begun so well. First contact came midmorning, with a knock on the front door. She'd gone to answer it, asking "who?" all the time knowing Corky was the one. Only there was no reply. She called again, "Yes?" and still silence.

Now, a little edgy. There was a tiny hole in the door, a protective device through which you could see who was standing there without opening. She peeked out.

No one was standing there. It was empty space.

But someone was knocking at the door again.

If it had been midnight, she would have been scared. Daylight was courage-making, so she said "Not funny" and threw open the door.

Only it was. Fats was sitting way down on the step, holding a bunch of fresh-picked weeds in his hand. His lips didn't move, but his voice came from around the corner of the house, saying "Roses for you, my dear."

Corky stepped into view. "He insisted on giving you those; he thinks they're roses." He picked Fats up.

"They *are* roses, schmucko."

"Humor him," Corky whispered. "It's best; he's scratchy before his morning coffee."

"Thank you," Peg said, taking the weeds.

"'Before my *morning coffee*,'" Fats said with undisguised emphasis.

"I'm sorry—sometimes I'm slow—would you by any chance like some instant?"

"I hadn't thought of it till now," Fats told her. "But why not, why not." They followed her into the house. "You know," Fats explained, "if you plant those carefully, they grow into oak trees—"

"—jerk, you're thinking of *acorns*," Corky said.

Fats shook his head. "Life's not so simple in the country."

"*You're* pretty simple in the country," Corky said.

"A *joke*, listen to that—schmucko made a funny, wonders must be ceasing."

They went into the kitchen and Peg managed to get the water boiled without once coming close to burning herself.

All the earmarks of a good day.

They chatted a lot through coffee, mostly just her and Corky, with occasionally Fats throwing in a zinger, but Corky didn't really need too much help, he was kind of on, not so quiet, not so shy.

They split when coffee cooled, Corky taking Fats back to the cabin to work on routines or whatever, but not before she'd invited him up for lunch if he wanted. And he seemed to.

But that meant there had to *be* lunch, which meant the trip into Normandy. She bought some luncheon meat, put it back, picked up some cold roast beef instead, put *that* back and decided to risk a chef's salad. And in case he wanted dinner, a couple of steaks, and frozen peas and nice frozen fries to go along. She stopped at Baskin-Robbins so the brownies and the pie could both be a la mode, in case he liked it that way, always assuming, of course, he was even there at all.

Lunch and supper cared for, she was on her way back before she did a U (illegal) and headed for the liquor store. She had enough for a bottle of Scotch and three bottles of a nice French wine. That gave her the idea for French bread, so back she went to the market, and got a loaf that was two feet long, a waste, but if he was there and if he was hungry, it would go, assuming, of course, he liked French bread at all.

What with one thing and another shopping took a while. She didn't get back to the cabins till quarter of one, didn't call Corky till half past. Lunch was successful, and so was the wine. They finished an entire bottle just before three.

Just before three was when the magic began.

She was the one who began it. She could not remember feeling that good that early in she didn't want to think how long, and she'd always loved tricks, so she asked him if he'd brought any.

"I don't do tricks."

"But you're a magician."

"Yeah, but, I don't know, tricks are like when I set up something—a fake deck of cards or a box with a false lid. It means some kind of secret preparation no one's supposed to know about. I don't work that way."

"You use whatever's available?"

Corky nodded. "In a club I have to use my own stuff because people just don't walk around with decks of cards."

"Coins though; everybody has them."

"I guess."

"Can you do magic with coins?"

Corky waggled his hand. "I ain't Leipzig," he said, and when she looked puzzled, added, "he was the master when it came to coins."

"I didn't know it was so specialized."

"Listen, there are thimble nuts—guys who spend their whole lives mainly on that. Cigarette guys. You kind of have to be a little weird to be a magician."

Peg got her wallet out of her purse. "Okay; fool me."

Corky lit a cigarette; inhaled. "I didn't know I was going to have to sing for my supper." He went over, sat on the living room couch, brought an ashtray, put it on the coffee table.

Peg came over, sat beside him. "Here's a quarter. Be wonderful."

"That all? Thanks a lot."

Peg watched him. He hesitated, holding the quarter in his right hand. She took one of his cigarettes, lit it, waited.

"I'm trying to think what might be a good way to begin," Corky said.

She sat, inhaling deeply. The cigarette tasted wonderful after all the wine. Sometimes they tasted like hay, but this one was worth the cancer scare. She inhaled again, and then started looking around because Corky had been smoking but now he wasn't, and the ashtray was empty, and she didn't want her very best piece of furniture catching fire.

"Okay," Corky said, "I've got it. Could I have a coin please?"

"I gave you the quarter."

"No, you said you would but you didn't."

She looked at his right hand. He hadn't moved it or done anything else. But the coin was gone. Peg watched as he inhaled on his cigarette. Funny, she thought, he's smoking again.

"Have you started doing things yet?"

"I can't very well do anything until I have something to do it with. Let me have a quarter, huh?"

She gave him a quarter.

And his cigarette was gone. Peg glanced at the empty ashtray.

"If you haven't got a quarter, give me a dime."

She looked. The second quarter was gone. And he was smoking again.

"Oh you bastard, you have too started."

"What?" He looked very innocent.

Peg started to laugh.

"If you'd ever give me a coin and I flipped it all the way to the ceiling and had it land on edge on the coffee table, that would be incredible, wouldn't you agree?"

"Do it, do it."

"I don't know how to do it," Corky told her. "I told you, I'm not an expert with coins. I think you're sitting on the quarters maybe."

Peg got up. The quarters were on the sofa cushion. She looked at Corky. His cigarette was gone. She picked up the quarters, handed them to him. He was smoking again. "Oh wow, that's wonderful."

"If I ever get around to doing anything, maybe it will be." He put the cigarette out in the ashtray, reached over, pulled a quarter from her ear. Then he found another on top of her head. He took them back, closed his fist, blew on it, asked her to stand again. The quarters were back beneath her on the sofa cushion.

Then he *really* started putting on a show. Peg just sat there staring because she'd loved magic since she was a kid, loved being fooled but knowing it was all going to come out right if you just waited, and after a little she went and got more wine, opening the second bottle, pouring a large glass for each of them, and she put all the change from her purse on the table, nickels and pennies and dimes, and he picked them up idly, talking about whether or not he should try the Sympathetic Coins sleight or maybe Thieves and Sheep would be easier and each time he suggested something he would argue himself out of it because he wasn't really secure on all the moves and while he was talking the coins seemed to fly, appearing and disappearing and reappearing, jumping from place to place as if they were doing it on their own because he certainly didn't seem to be doing anything to help them, just sitting there trying to figure out what to do, always deciding against doing anything at all because he could try the Tenkia Exchange, sure, any jerk could *try* it but any jerk could goof it too, so that was a no-no and maybe the Waiter's Tip would impress her but not if he blew the flip, if that happened she'd probably laugh at his fumbling, so finally what he decided to do was nothing at all, he really wasn't a coin man, he'd never really been into coins enough for public consumption, and while he went into his final apology he went into a double roll and Peg stared as the two quarters walked across the back of Corky's hands—they seemed almost to be doing that, walking, as they went from the second finger across the middle to the ring, then around the pinkie and under on the thumb, the back to the index again, chasing each other around his hands in a final wondrous flourish and he was done.

Peg just sat there.

Corky got up, walked to the window that overlooked the lake, stared down in the direction of his cabin.

"Have you ever considered a career in magic?" Peg said. Corky glanced over at her, smiled.

Peg watched him. He was looking down toward his cabin again. "Is it getting late for you again? You have to leave?"

"Of course not."

"Then listen, I know magicians never tell and all that, but how do you do that stuff?"

"If you really thought, you'd figure it. People just don't much want to know the truth. If they did, we'd all be out of business."

"I don't know how you did that with the cigarette—sometimes you were smoking, sometimes it was gone, and you never once moved your hands up to your mouth."

"If I tell you just the one, can we change the subject?"

Peg waited.

Corky lowered his voice slightly. "That looked like a real cigarette, but actually it was rolled in vanishing paper, you inhale on it a certain way, it gets invisible—I don't do that one a lot because the paper costs a fortune, you have to cure it for weeks to get it to disappear properly. If you buy the cheap kind, instead of getting invisible it turns green."

"You're really a crumb."

"Think."

"C'mon, Corky, you said you'd tell me."

"Changed my mind; you do the telling. If it isn't invisible and I don't use my hands, where could it go?"

"Your mouth? You just zap it inside and leave it there, burning and all? That's got to be it."

"It's called tonguing," Corky explained. "It's a technique. Like everything else in magic."

"My God, doesn't it burn?"

"You can singe yourself pretty good when you're learning, I'll admit that."

"When you say everything, you don't mean *everything*. Like sword swallowers don't really swallow swords."

"Sure they do."

"Don't they get sick to their stomachs?"

"They do that too. If they keep *on* getting sick to their stomachs, they generally tend to drift into another occupation."

"Nerts," Peg said.

"This shouldn't bother you. You were the one who asked about knowing secrets in the first place."

"Can you explain everything?"

"Pretty much."

"Pretty much isn't the same as everything though—what's there you can't explain?"

"You mean what do I know about that's 'magic'—impossible, something that couldn't happen but did?"

Peg nodded, turned her wineglass.

"Hey, I'd really like changing the subject. Right here."

"How come?"

"Magic's to entertain—you don't take it seriously. Don't look for more than's there."

"And you think I'm doing that?"

"I think."

"I'm really not, I'm having a very good time, it's just that I get bugged when—" She gestured outside. It was already beginning to darken slightly. Peg looked at her watch. "Three-twenty and the shadows getting longer."

From somewhere in the surrounding woods now, another cry from the cat.

"Probably got himself a grizzly," Corky said.

"Tell me about the impossible thing, please?"

Corky came back to the couch, picked up a couple of coins, began fiddling them around. "Okay, briefly. I'll thumbnail it and then over and out, deal?"

"'Course."

"I didn't see this, I wasn't there, ordinarily I would never believe it, except it was Merlin told me."

"Who?"

"Merlin, Jr. He was my teacher. I guess I kind of worshiped him, if that doesn't sound too unmanly."

"What was the impossible thing?"

"First," Corky said, and he made a flourish; "the mystery of the Alchemist's Coin."

"Do that later—come on—why are you putting me off?"

Corky spun the coins on the table. "Because I don't know where this is going, and it's bad for magicians when they don't feel in control."

"Just stop worrying so much."

Corky started talking very fast. "Merlin was a great artist, as good as the game, and I know you've never heard of him but that's because he wasn't successful, not because he didn't have the skills—he was ugly, see; fierce-looking. Big, powerful. He frightened people. Kids mostly. He scraped all his life. It made him tough. He was a hard man, you better believe that. So when he told me about this, even though I knew it was bullshit, I wasn't so sure it was bullshit, if you follow."

Peg had her wineglass in her hands now, fingers locked.

"I never knew his wife, but he adored her. He called her his 'dumpling'—you can't believe how weird that sounded, this giant of a ferocious guy with this dopey tone coming into his voice whenever he talked about his 'dumpling.' I've seen her picture. She had a sweet face, pretty as hell, at least for those days, and this blimp body. A tub. They made some colorful team, I guess—they worked together in his act—him with this hussar's face and her looking like a Shirley Temple doll perched on a barrel. Anyway, that's the cast of characters, the two of them."

"And the impossible thing?"

"He claimed he could read her mind."

The coins started dancing over Corky's fingers again. "Not all the time. And not often. But toward the end, the days before she died, that's when he said it happened."

"You really believe it, don't you?"

Corky shrugged, the coins stopped parading. "I'm not sure. I guess I want to." He shivered. "I'd love a fire."

"Finish up, then we'll have one."

"Nothing to finish. Merlin and his wife, when they were

doing their act, they used to include the standard telepathy crap, with cards mostly, all the fake stuff that works best in the small towns. Then, toward the end, in the hospital, they began passing the time with this and that and they tried it for real. It never worked until just before the cancer got her. The week she died it happened. He always blamed himself for that—he never wanted it badly enough to happen before. He never concentrated enough to try and grab onto what she was trying to send him. Those last days they both wanted it enough; wanted to touch each other enough, was how he put it. They were desperate for something to remember."

Peg finished her wine, poured some more. She filled Corky's glass too. "Do you know how they did it? I mean, the exact procedures and everything."

"Sure."

"How?"

"Why?"

"Interested is all."

"Well I'm not and I'd really like a fire."

"I have lots of cards."

"I told you already, I don't want to get into this."

"We're not getting into anything, Corky; we're just two old acquaintances passing the time."

"That's not so and you know it."

"Let me just get the cards. It'll be fun."

"You want me to try it."

"Why would that be so terrible?"

"*Because I'd fail.*"

"Don't get so all hot and bothered. You wouldn't be the first; people fail all the time."

"You wouldn't like it."

"Oh, Corky, I wouldn't care."

"Believe me on this."

"Are you afraid?"

"Of course I'm afraid."

"Of what, dummy?"

Corky drank half his wine. "Let's just say I don't want you thinking bad of me."

"But I wouldn't."

"Good. You say so, I believe you, let's not push it."

"I can't conceive of me ever thinking bad of you—frankly, the only thing that might upset me is if you wouldn't try, because that would show you didn't trust me when I said I was only interested in a little fun."

"I'm under enough pressure without this. I'm trying to get away from pressure, that's why I'm here, I told you all that."

"I think we should forget the whole thing."

"Don't use that tone, please, Peg."

"You're already mind reading me, aren't you."

"Don't use that tone, please, Peg."

"All I said was let's forget it."

"But you don't mean that."

"Look at him," Peg said. "Mind reading me again."

Corky finished his wine.

There was a long pause.

"Well, what do you want to talk about now," Peg said, finally.

"If you're going to disapprove of me, I guess it doesn't matter if I fail or not, get the cards."

She got up right away, went for the foyer closet where the cards always were, wondering why she was acting this way, making him do something, why was she being so bitchy. She wasn't, almost never, it wasn't her way.

But you are now, she thought as she opened the closet door, started to rummage around. "Any special kind of deck, color or anything?"

"Any two."

She grabbed contrasting bicycles, a red and a black, brought them to the coffee table, put them down. "How did this Merlin do it?" she asked.

"Shuffle both the decks. Get the jokers out if there are any."

There were. She put them aside. "Now shuffle?"

"First one, then the other."

She shuffled, and he sat beside her watching her do it. When she was done she waited.

"Which deck do you want, red or black?"

She surprised herself and picked black.

"The red one's mine then; push it away from you and leave it there."

She did.

He got up and walked away, his back to her. His back still turned, he stopped. "All right, pick a card from your deck."

She reached in, came up with the ten of hearts. "Okay."

"Now look at it."

"I did."

"You must really look at it."

"I'm looking, Jesus, don't get mad at me." Ten of hearts, ten of hearts; she repeated it half a dozen times to herself. "Ready."

"Put it on the pack and cut the pack."

Peg did.

"Cut it again, cut it half a dozen times if you want. Then square it up."

She decided three cuts were enough. Then she made the pack neat. "Ready for orders."

"Take my pack."

She picked up the red one.

"Go through it till you find the same card in my pack, then take it out."

She found his ten of hearts.

"When you're done, put my pack away, just keep the one card."

When she was finished she said, "What's going to happen now?"

"Tell me what's happened so far."

"Well, I got out the cards and I shuffled both decks and I picked the deck I wanted and I picked the card I wanted and I cut the cards after that."

"And where was I?"

"Standing with your back turned."

Corky turned around and faced her. "Well, that's kind of it. What happened next was Merlin took his wife's pack with the card in and she held the card from his pack, and she put it next to her heart and cleared her mind except whatever that card was and he went through her pack trying to pick up her card and those last few days, he was able to."

"What's my card?"

"I don't know—I've got a one in fifty-two chance of guessing. The reason you go through all the rigmarole—*your* cards, *you* doing all the work, *me* with my back turned—that's so if it works you know it really did, no one can question any—"

"I'm thinking of my card," Peg said. Ten of hearts, ten, ten, keep thinking of the ten, Peggy old girl, ten ten ten of hearts ten of hearts. "What is it?"

Corky looked embarrassed. "Sorry."

"Well you're not concentrating, pick up my pack, go through it like you're supposed to."

He reached over, picked up her pack, looked at the faces of the cards, going through them one at a time.

Peg put the card by her left breast and closed her eyes wondering why she wanted this so badly, she hadn't the foggiest, but she did, she did want it.

Very badly.

Ten, dammit please, ten of hearts, Christ, just say ten of hearts, Corky, I'm thinking so hard of the ten of hearts the ten of hearts the ten of hearts *say it.*

She opened her eyes.

"Nothing," Corky said.

Peg stared at him and pushed the card harder against her body and thought of nothing but the card, the one card, the ten, the red ten *the red goddam ten of goddam hearts.*

She saw the expression hit his face, and then he was whispering, ". . . omijesus it's red, isn't it? . . ."

"I—I wouldn't know, it might be, maybe not, go on." She started to close her eyes again.

"No," Corky managed. "We must watch each other. And you've got to think harder than you ever thought about anything because I want this to happen now Peg and it will. I know it's red, I saw the color in my mind now look at me and please think."

Peg thought. Ten, ten don't think of anything else but the ten, the heart ten, it must be the heart ten, if it isn't the ten of hearts get rid of it, banish it, make him see the ten of hearts—

"—you're not thinking."

"I am!"

"Harder then," and now he was starting to perspire.

Peg looked into his eyes, they were nice eyes, Corky's brown, sure, but they had a nice shape, they were friendly and gentle and—

"—HARDER!"

Omigod, I wasn't thinking about it at all, I'm sorry, sorry, please, don't guess what I was doing then, I was wandering, your eyes don't matter only the ten of hearts matters the ten of hearts the ten the ten please God the ten of hearts the ten of hearts I WANT THIS.

"Yes."

Ten of hearts, ten ten ten ten—

"Yes."

Ten hearts heart ten heart ten heart ten heart heart omigod, he's got it, he's got it! *I can see it in his eyes.*

"Turn . . ." his voice was very dry. "Turn over your card, please." They showed their cards at the same exact time.

She turned over the ten of hearts.

He turned over . . . the diamond deuce.

For a minute Peg was really surprised, she'd been that sure, but then she realized it was ridiculous, the whole thing was ridiculous, feeling hurt and upset was ridiculous, and disappointed, he was human, that's all anybody was, and she said, "Hey that was fun," and her tone was convincing as she quickly stood, said, "I'll just see about some wood for a fire now" and started to stand.

It was 3:35.

And Corky started acting crazy.

"That . . ." he said, and he strung the word out long—"was your fault all your fault," and now the words were run together.

"What was?" She was standing by the couch now.

"Sit back down Peg you will sit back down." Again the words ran together.

Only this time he was rubbing his left temple as he spoke.

And his left eye was beginning to blink.

"Let me just get the fire—"

"—*get your ass back down!*" and he reached out, spun her around to the couch again.

Roughly.

"You didn't think enough. You started to do fine, I got the red fine, but then you decided not to go any further, isn't that so?"

She watched him pacing around and around, small circles, as if in some kind of round cell. The blinking was worse.

"Why did you do that to me, Peg?"

"Do what?"

"You made me try that with the cards. I knew I couldn't get it right but you made me try. And then when I was close you didn't think hard enough. You humiliated me, Peg, and I want to know why."

"Corky, my God, it was nothing, a trick—"

"—I don't do tricks. You think bad of me, don't you?"

"No, of—"

"—you're disappointed in me. Tell the truth, I know the truth so you might as well tell it."

After a while she nodded. "A little maybe. I wanted that to happen, I guess."

"You wanted it—don't you know what it meant to me?—if *I* could have made it happen it would have proved that no matter what any man said to you, no matter how many lies, whatever I'd said you'd have believed, because we'd have proved it, just like Merlin did, if you care for someone enough, if you want something enough and you care, you can make it happen."

"Can I get up now?"

"No. I was in bad shape back in New York, Peg."

"You said."

"Terrible shape—"

She nodded; he was rubbing his temple harder now. Peg shivered from the cold.

"I had to run but where do you go when there's no place to go, you go home. Only I didn't have a real home, but Father, you know he worked at the G so I thought, I'll start there, I'll backtrack to where I was okay and try and do it right this time, only when I got up here I thought, Jesus Christ, your father was nothing to you, he never even looked at you, so I stopped here, I had the driver take a shortcut and it brought me past here because I wanted to find out what had happened to you, where you were living, what country, what world, how many kids, anything. I came here because I wanted a good piece of news about Peggy Ann Snow, I've loved you all my goddam life, you never once thought bad of me, when I was growing up, you were the only one. And you never did till now."

"I don't think bad of you."

"Disappointed. You said that."

"All right, I did, true, but only for a little, I don't anymore, true, I feel terrible I mean that, but Jesus, I'd been alone, you were the first person in days I'd talked to, you always had a crush on me, it was flattering. It was then it is now only now you've gone and made a success of yourself and I didn't, my marriage didn't work, there's no kids, my life's been shit, Corky, and it was very romantic, being able to be so close you could tell without talking."

"This time it won't be your fault," Corky said then.

Peg looked at him.

"We're going to do it right this time, Peg. I know that." He would not stop staring at her. "We both want it enough. It's going to be fine."

"What if it isn't? Fine."

"I know. You have to trust me. When people are desperate for something to happen it can happen if they're desperate enough and I am, we are, both of us, Merlin did it and so can we."

"How . . . upset will you be if you miss?"

"I won't."

"But if you do?"

"Very. But I won't. Shuffle the cards, Peg. Do everything just like before."

She shuffled, took the black deck again, picked—the three of clubs this time—put it back on top, cut, cut, cut again, then another time, squared her cards. She picked the three of clubs from his pack, held it to her heart.

Corky sat beside her on the couch. He'd had his eyes closed from before she picked her card. Now he went through her deck in silence.

Peg thought of the three of clubs. Thought of it hard. Then she began thinking about what would happen when it didn't work—*if* it didn't—would he get more strange, start acting crazier, or would they just do it and do it, spending their lives trying to get the right card from one mind to another. "Are we gonna do this until we get it right?" she asked.

"Don't talk." He was staring at her eyes now.

"But are we?"

"I told you. It's going to happen now. This time. But you must think."

"I'm thinking."

"No. I can tell from your eyes. You're not."

Well, maybe that wasn't much of a mind read but it was at least accurate. It would be nice if he could—when he got it right. Correction. It will be nice when he gets it right. It was nice that he loved her, that hadn't happened to her in a while —she should never really have left high school, it had been downhill all the way since then. What was my card? Right, three of clubs, three of clubs, the ever-loving trey.

"Why are you afraid? You're not thinking."

They were staring at each other harder now. "I didn't want you getting more upset."

"I'm not upset anymore. I'm very serene, Peg. I'm confident and you should be confident because we are special people, and special people belong with each other—"

"—yes—"

"—are you thinking?—"

"—not like I should—"

"—but you will?—"

"—now—" she nodded, still staring, still watching his nice eyes set in his sweet face, the eyes of someone who loved her, who loved her, and wanted to prove it, that's all this was really, just—three—proving that you cared for someone—three of clubs—and that nothing else mattered, just—three of clubs—three of clubs—his eyes are burning, pinning me down—making me—three of clubs—making me helpless and pinning—three of clubs—three of clubs, in all the world there is only the three of clubs, the three of clubs, the three the three, the black club three, the club the club club club three club three three three three club three club three club three clubthree clubthree clubthree clubthree . . .

". . . three of clubs . . ." Corky whispered.

Numbly, she put it down, nodded.

Corky sat back, looked about to cry.

Nothing really important happened then until about five till four, when Ben Greene the Postman came knocking.

6

Corky was out back by the kitchen, bringing in a supply of wood for the fire and never heard the first raps. Peg said, "Who is it?" and when the answering "Greene" sounded friendly enough, she opened the door. "We're kind of closed," she said to the tiny bald man in the probably tan cashmere overcoat.

"Thriving wasn't the adjective I would apply to your enterprise. Would you tell Mr. Withers the Postman—I happen to be his representative—has come to fetch him."

Peg just looked at him.

"*Fräulein*, I don't seem to be getting through to you. Is it a matter of your thickness or my ineptitude?"

"You're kind of funny," Peg said.

"I'll show you my reviews someday: 'riotous'—Atkinson, *Times*. Get Corky, huh, I'm not doing my aging bohunkus much good out here."

"I went to high school with Corky Withers," Peg said. "Whyever do you think he's here?"

"*Know* he's here."

"You haven't answered."

"Because, *signorina*, a very corrupt and eager young taxi driver called me and asked was I Corky's agent and I asked him how he found that out and he said, 'I caught his act on the *Merv Griffin* show and I called them and asked who his agent was and they said you.'"

"I'm sure this is all very interesting, Mr. Greene, but I'm trying to get the place ready for sale and—"

"—you are wrong, my pigeon, what I have thus far explained is *not* interesting, but it gets that way, so have patience. This young and corrupt cabdriver says to me, 'You can rest easy, he's safe.' 'Safe?' say I. 'Safe where?' And he replies, 'He bribed me not to tell and I could never break my word, not when a guy's given me an extra hundred.' By now, since I have been dealing with charlatans since my early days when I handled Rasputin on his Russian tour, I knew exactly what had to be done and who had to do it. I doubled Corky's bribe, salved the cabbie's conscience with soft words about it all being for everybody's own good, met him in front of my apartment, exchanged cash for whereabouts. Those whereabouts, according to my informant, are where we fence at this moment."

"Gee I'm sorry," Peg said. "But I haven't seen Corky in what must be fifteen years."

The Postman nodded.

"If I do though, I'll be sure and say you're looking for him, Mr. Greene."

The Postman laughed. "Somehow that misses being reassuring. If he hasn't come for fifteen years, why would he change habits now?"

Peg shrugged.

The Postman didn't go, just watched her.

"Probably that cab man was lying," Peg said.

The Postman went into his Jolson routine. "Somebody sho' am."

"Whatever," Peg said. Then: "Good-bye."

"Until we meet again might be more accurate," he replied, and then he turned, his disbelief open, and took a few small steps away.

"Were you a friend of his or something?" Peg called.

"Why does that matter?"

"You haven't answered me again."

"I was a good acquaintance, but my question still stands."

"Because he's under a lot of pressure and I wouldn't want anybody but a friend to see him."

"He's here then?"

"Was. He came in yesterday afternoon not long before dark. I was kind of a school pal. He asked could he spend the night in one of the cabins and I thought 'why not?' even though we're kind of closed. We had a big night last night—hours of talking, school stuff. He told me he was being pressured bad. He seemed nervous I thought."

"He was fine with me when we talked in person—but then he did this disappearing act. He's a very delicate mechanism; that happens with talent."

"See, on account of this pressure, I don't think he'd want anyone but friends to be with him. I don't want to sound conceited but I think all the talking we did about the old days, that made him feel better."

"You're an undeniable morsel, and I can't imagine you having an adverse effect on the general public."

"It didn't last though is the thing. This morning he was all edgy again. Upset about whatever it is that's going on back in the city."

"When did he leave?"

"I had to go into town to get some stuff for my husband. Corky asked would I take him to the G. Grossinger's."

The Postman nodded. "Being an agent, I suspected what the G was."

"Corky didn't have much luggage. Just the two pieces. I drove him over. His father used to work there. Rubdowns. Stuff like that. If you want to know what I think, Mr. Greene, I think Corky's going after his past. I looked up one of my dream analysis paperbacks—"

"—he told you his dreams?"

"No, but those are the only kind of books I have that talk about when you're whacked up. He's at the G now, but I'm guessing he's going upstate."

"Why?"

"'Cause he said something in passing about his mother and how he'd never visited her grave. His mother was from the Binghamton area."

The old man made a face and rubbed his bald head. "Binghamton, Jesus. That's all I needed." He started away again, then stopped. "When you dropped him off, did he say he'd get back in touch with you, anything?"

"Nothing like that. The usual 'thanks' and 'take cares' and when he was out of the car, he came around to my side and I rolled down the window and he said, 'I'll tell you something crazy. All my life I fought to get successful and you know what? Success is a failure.'"

"Performers." The Postman shook his head. "Would you believe I was once six-foot-six, blond, and I'm only thirty years old? It's dealing with performers that's made me what I am."

Peg smiled.

The Postman sighed. "Back to the chase." He looked up at Peg. "May I tell you something? The first part of our talk, you were not convincing. You're a rotten liar, I like you much better like now, when a few truths get thrown around."

"I just didn't want anyone bad going after Corky."

The Postman pushed his old body into an attempted bow. "Joy to thee and me," he said, and then he left.

Peg stood in the doorway watching until he was gone. Still facing out, she said, "How much did you hear?"

From inside: Corky. "I think all."

"What did you think?"

"Binghamton was an inspiration."

Peg broke out laughing.

"Hey."

"Huh?"

"I owe you."

Peg stared out at the edge of the sun. "Something will come to me."

7

They made love for the first time early that evening. She came down to his cabin and asked could she come in and he said it's unlocked and she said the weather report is for cold so I brought you a sweater and he said thanks but they both knew it was bullshit.

He wondered how cold did they say it might get and she answered she couldn't quite remember but pretty and he said again, thanks, and tried the sweater on and she said seems to fit okay and he said feels warm too as the bullshit continued.

She told him it was Duke's and he said the sweater and she shrugged yeah and he said well that was thoughtful of him even if he doesn't know it and she said well that was always a strong point of his and he said good old Duke and she shrugged yeah again and he wondered if he grabbed for her what if she rejected him, better not to try and she hesitated too long before turning to go which led him to think otherwise, it was worth the gamble so he grabbed and they embraced and Christ it was clumsy but when they broke she didn't try going anywhere, only laughed a little and he said is that at me and she told him no, at me, I was gonna say we mustn't and then I thought dummy, that's why you came down here in the first place so they embraced again, not so clumsily this time.

They walked in silence past the curtained kitchenette toward the little bedroom and still in that silence, started taking off their clothes, and Corky knew he should be caressing her or at least keeping the conversational ball somehow going but his three fears shut him up so they just went on, the silence building, their clothes piling garment on top of garment. His

first fear was the least of his worries, that after all his day-
dreams, she wouldn't measure up, the body only seen before
in fantasy wasn't fifteen and things happened to you, gravity
and disappointment etch and change you, but when he finally
turned and faced her, both of them without clothing, the first
fear went and then she moved into his arms as the second fear
took hold, that he would be incompetent, lacking in sexual
power, but that fear disappeared as they lay together on the
bed and he went inside her which left the third fear only, that
he would explode instantly, or soon thereafter, and then there
would be that awful colloquy that was really the male na-
tional anthem:

> 'i'm sorry'
> 'listen, it's all right'
> 'no, i'm really sorry'
> 'don't be'
> 'i feel like such a jerk'
> 'you did fine'
> 'you mean that?'
> 'would i lie to you?'

But many minutes later they were still locked and rhythmic,
and the third fear vanished leaving Corky with nothing but
the realization that what he wished for he was getting, which
didn't happen to everybody, not every day, for there he was,
deep within Peggy Ann Snow and wherever her body went on
the bed, he followed her with his, firmly, gracefully, all of it
proving only that sometimes, when you really needed Him,
God put in an appearance after all.

In the next room, in the overstuffed chair, eyes wide, sat
Fats, his head slightly turned, as if listening.

"I'll bet they don't give service like *that* at Grossinger's,"
Peg said, inevitably, later.
Corky lay quietly, his arms around her.
"That was more fun even than a Tupperware party."

Corky smiled.

"Drop in again in fifteen years."

"Why the jokes?"

"I'm kind of feeling my way along, I never played around before. True, I'm not claiming that I'm so pure and virtuous, I just never gave that much of a damn. Sex wasn't a big thing in my family; I don't think my mother was ever absolutely positive what her vagina was for. That's what my old man used to indicate, anyway."

"What about Duke?"

"Mainly he blows in my ear a lot."

Corky started laughing.

"True."

"How come?"

"I deceived him into thinking it drives me mad; I feel crummy about that sometimes. He's tonguing away and I'm doing my best to moan while I think about shopping lists. I can be a very crappy lady if I put my mind to it."

"Why'd you fake in the first place?"

"Ah. I've done a lot of thinking about that and you've got to remember that when I graduated from high school, there were nine different guys who claimed they were boffing me regular. Here I was, eighteen years old, undeniably the town pump, and still virgin. So I had a very good inkling that my future didn't have me sticking here in Normandy. Off to college. Dumb. Not so much that maybe, as distracted. One semester and now I'm off to be a stew. Bad move. I'm terrific on the ground, in the air, not so hot. Shuffle off to Buffalo. Doctor's assistant. Give shots, console, and I'm really not bad. But big city life isn't for me. Back to Normandy. Twenty-two now. Getting a little long in the tooth. Dah-dum: in his white charger, comes Duke. Drives a Lincoln, looks like Elvis, due to take over his old man's real estate office and his old man is *old*. We date. Hints, lots of sex talk. He's confident. He knows, according to him anyway, his women. No real moves. Still hints. Chitchat. But he's getting interested in me. I give him that. Once he cared plenty. So, as it must happen, we arrive in his apartment one night alone. This move, that fake. I wasn't all that in the market. He can sense I'm not succumbing. Proposes. Will I tie the knot? Well lemme tell ya, that was the best offer I'd had that day. Not so terrible being married to a rising young executive that looks like Elvis Presley. And then, in desperation, he's going to it with my ear. It was so sad I didn't know whether to laugh or fake it, but I knew if I laughed, it was Elvis g'bye. So I moaned and eventually spread and a couple eventualities after that, we got married and Duke's old man died on schedule, and there he was, his own man at twenty-five, and in less than five years he managed, with no help from anyone, to not only go bankrupt but bald." She kissed Corky on the mouth. "Now you know all my secrets. Fair is fair. Tell me a sex story back."

"I don't even have to think. It's not even much of a story."

"If it's not juicy, forget it. If I go to hell for this, I want it all to've been worth it."

"Shut up. It's not long. Freshman year, the end of class, the teacher is calling us up to hand in our homework assignments. I was just sitting there, not a thought to my name. That's what's so incredible. I went from zero to sixty and no time passed."

"I don't get you."

"What I mean is, I wasn't thinking about cards or coins or anything. Just a kid waiting for class to be done. I'd handed in my paper. If I had an emotion, it was just bored. Getting on in the day. Okay, now you've got to picture this. The teacher calls for this broad's paper and she gets up and walks to the front. And I'm watching. And as she walked, she passed *between* me and the outside sun. That's important. The sun is *behind* her. I'm still watching remember. And this girl walks past me. She's wearing a white sweater. And the sweater bulges out some in the front, because this one is kind of stacked. And as she passes me, I realized this amazing thing: the sweater bulged out, but with the sun behind her, I could see through the thing, and I could see her breasts curving back. You get it? I was just thirteen and *I saw this girl's breasts*. I don't want to oversell it, but my heart—I mean this— it pounded. From nothing to sixty—it just started smashing around inside me. It was the most powerful thing I think I ever saw in my life."

"Why?"

"Because that was the first moment I knew what my cock was for. I understood it earlier, but that was the *second* that I realized the world had changed and it wasn't ever going back. To this day, I can tell you everything about that room and the sun and the color white the sweater was."

"I guess that's kind of sweet," Peg said.

"It was you, dummy; that was you walking past me in French class."

"Well why didn't you say that before; now it all makes good sense. The sight of my boobs would unhinge anybody permanent." She paused a moment. "Was it really me?"

"Oh yes."

"That's just terrific."

"*I* thought so."

"I'll tell you the truth, Cork. Things have sure no shit changed a little around here since yesterday afternoon." She rolled her body gently against his. "What exectly do you call what we've been doing?"

"Fokking," Corky told her.

"I think it may catch on," Peg said. "Let's do it until we get it right."

"I don't think I'm ready."

She touched him. "Surprise."

Corky stood in the living room, called out to the kitchen, "How come you have all these same kind of books?"

"Which?"

"Two weeks to learn this, thirty days to build that."

"That's my self-help collection. I'm an addict." Corky walked out into the kitchen. Peg was unwrapping the frozen peas and fries. "It's how come I speak funny—my grammar sucks but I can spell 'antediluvian.' It's a-n-t-*e* not a-n-t-*i*. I forgot what it means though. Right now I'm into creating a better memory."

"Why're you such a self-helper?"

Peg shrugged. "I started a couple years ago, when I realized no one else was gonna give me a hand."

"Want mine?" Corky held out his right.

She kissed it, touched the fingers to her cheek. "Don't think I'm not appreciative, but I'm a basket case in the kitchen—should I put the steak in first or start to warm the French bread? That's why I like one-dish meals; it's the only way I can get everything to come out together."

In a very corny voice, Corky said, "Let me take you away from all this, Madeleine."

"Oh Cuthbert, dare we?" She picked up the French fry wrapper, reread the instructions.

Seriously, Corky said, "Seriously."

"Huh?"

"Let's take off. I got a lot of money with me. We could go no place and stay awhile. Just us."

"I should dump Duke and you'd leave Fats, is that your offer?"

"That's exactly my offer—it's not so crazy—you don't care a crap for Duke—he probably wouldn't even realize you'd gone from what you say about him. And I wouldn't work on my act. See, that's why Fats is helpful, practice, to stay on top of things, but today, when I did those coin sleights for you, all that patter about should I try this stunt or that and deciding against it *while I was doing it*—I never came up with that kind of thing before you—you give me confidence, Peg—I don't need anything else around—I could do maybe a whole different kind of thing if you were around for support—maybe I wouldn't need Fats at all, I could kind of please people on my own."

"You're on your own when you're with Fats."

"Of course I am, *I* know that, but the audience, see, they think Fats is the funny one—really—people laugh at him putting me down."

"I'm guilty of that, I admit it."

"I'm the talent though—that's the real truth of it but now I'm gonna tell you something that's gonna rock you—sometimes even I get to think that Fats is the talent. Without him and those wisecracks, I'm just another schlepper. I didn't feel that way with you though. When I was making those coins dance, that was *me* getting the smile. Let's not make more of a deal out of it than it is. Peg, I'm just saying, throw away the first thirty years of your life and come wiz me to zee Kazz-bah."

"That's very sweet, I appreciate it, it's probably only the best offer I've had all decade, but the answer has got to be no way, can't be, impossible."

It became improbable over the Scotch and water. While they rescued the French bread from the smoking oven, it moved to a distant but not inconceivable possibility. The steak was raw, but the offer she agreed to at least put on the back burner. It got to the front burner when they finished the wine. By the time Corky left after the Baskin-Robbins, she said she'd give an answer soon. That week, that night, who knew, she had to ponder. At the door, Corky kissed his own index finger, moved it to her nipples, touched them. He had seen something like that once in a French film and wondered at the time what it would feel like doing it to Peggy Ann Snow.

All in all, not bad.

"What'd'ya say, Sports Fans," Corky said as he walked into the cabin living room.

From the overstuffed chair, Fats just grunted.

Corky hung his jacket up in the living room closet. "What's up?"

"Kind of blue."

"About?"

"All this atmosfuckingphere has got me down."

"The country grows on you."

"So does cancer—hey pardner?"

"Speak."

"Ah thank the time has come fer you'n me to be moseyin' on. Let's haul ass, Shane."

"We will, we will."

"Our work is done here, Masked Man—there's no reason to stick around—and rustlers is causin' a ruckus in Dodge—"

"I said we'd go."

"I'm speaking of an imminent departure, schmucko—that's our bone of contention."

"Sorry," Corky said.

"I want to blow this crib, goddammit."

"Simmer down."

"What's so great here?—"

"—nothing, but—"

"—screw the 'buts'—I want *out*—"

"—*no* and that's it—"

"—listen, Laddie, there's no reason for us to have a confronfuckingtation over something as easy to solve as this: you want to stay, terrific, stay. Just get me back to New York. You come when you want."

Corky started unbuttoning his shirt.

"I take it your silence indicates a lack of enthusiasm for my suggestion."

"The discussion's over, period."

"I don't think I've been getting through to you—I want to hit New York in the forfuckingseeable future—"

"I told you before, just simmer the hell down—"

"—I won't—I won't—"

"—you will—"

"—*won't won't won't won't won't*—"

"—*will!*"

"—just because some bitch of an aging ingenue puts out for you—"

"—you watch it mister—"

" '—oh, Corky, you do it so good, oh Christ Corky, you are some hung stud, oh God don't stop—' "

"*You* stop! Right now—*or there's gonna be consequences!*—"

That was when Fats screamed.

Ashen and trembling, old eyes wide, the Postman stood staring from the doorway . . .

"How do you like it?" Corky said brightly. "I think it's gonna be terrific."

The Postman could only shake his head.

"I haven't got it to performance level yet, but it's got the potential to add a whole new dimension; at least I hope so."

"How long you been like this, kid?"

"Like what?" Corky started laughing. "Oh come on. You don't think that was for real? Christ, how do you think I rehearse?"

"No good."

"You been in the business half a century—how can you not tell a routine when you hear one?"

"Gangrene never was the brightest," Fats said.

"It's for the *act*—you're really getting senile, Postman— here's my reasoning: Fats insults me, I do tricks, Fats insults me, I do tricks—eventually that's got to get a little repetitive wouldn't you say? So what I decided to do was expand the format, add more give and take, increase the banter, use the sleights more for climax or punctuation. Lemme give you an example." He grabbed Fats, held him in position. "Ladies and gentlemen, for your viewing enjoyment, my version of The Miser's Dream."

"Was it a wet dream?" Fats wondered.

"No—shut up—ladies and gentlemen, imagine if you will—"

"—when I have a wet dream, all that happens is I wake up covered with sawdust," Fats said.

Corky looked at Fats. "If you don't stop interrupting, there's a Mafia woodpecker who'll go to work on you."

Fats looked at Corky. "I would like very much a wood pecker."

"Don't encourage him please, ladies and gentlemen—now, once there was a miser, and like many misers, this one had managed to secrete a fortune—"

"—I would trade my fortune for a penis."

"You haven't got a fortune."

"That's all right, I haven't got a penis either." Corky looked at the Postman.

The old man just shook his head. "Like I said already once, no good."

"I don't get it," Corky said. "What's going on in your head? How can you not see what great stuff I'm working up?"

"Is this why you wouldn't take the medical exam? You figured someone would find out?"

"Bullshit—I'll take the *stupid* exam—I just needed to get my head on straight; I was afraid of success, as close as I can figure. But now my mind's made up one hundred percent. I'll take the exam, do the show, whatever you want."

"What I want," the Postman answered, "is for you to see somebody."

"*See* somebody? Who would I see?"

"*Quit with the games!*"

"Quit the goddam yelling," Fats said.

"Shut up," Corky said.

"He shouldn't yell at you," Fats went on. "You been up here busting your hump coming up with new stuff for the act —that was blockbuster material, mister—when he says about the Mafia woodpecker and I come back with wanting a wood pecker, they'll *howl* in Vegas on that. That was major league *funny.*"

"Nothing's funny anymore," the Postman said, and he started for the door.

"What're you gonna do?" Corky said.

"Ask around. Make a few phone calls."

"Tell people, you mean."

"*Corky you're not in control*—yes I'm going to tell people— qualified people—we got to do what we can to help you."

"Put me in the hatch, that's what you're saying. You're so fucking old you can't tell a rehearsal from real conversation and on the strength of *eavesdropping*, you're going to spread the word that I'm bonkers."

"No one's going to spread any word. Whatever I do I do for your good, not mine. I just want to help you, kid."

"Somebody play 'Hearts and Flowers,'" Fats said.

"Close your goddam hole," Corky said.

"Butt me," Fats said.

"Listen, for just one second," Corky said to the Postman. "Don't you owe me that?"

The Postman nodded.

Corky gestured toward the couch. "Please."

The Postman sat.

"Got any of them jazzy see-gars?" Fats wondered.

"I *was* kind of out of control—back in the city—nothing loony tunes or anything, but I could feel myself beginning to come apart at the seams a little."

"So you took off."

"That's right," Corky said.

"And now you're telling me you're fine."

"That's right again."

The Postman sadly shook his head, rubbed his eyes.

"I owe it all to Peg is what you've got to understand," Corky said. "She makes everything different."

"The one with the knockers," Fats said.

"Shut up," Corky said.

"Just wanted the Postman to keep the cast of characters straight," Fats said. "Once you hit senility, two's company, three's impossible."

"I remember this Peg plenty well," the Postman said. "She sent me halfway to effing Binghamton."

"She was just trying to look out for me, protect me."

"Make your point, kid, it's closing time."

"Maybe I *was* too much with Fats, maybe I *did* take the act too serious, but I swear to you, I got a way out now. Peg. True. She *believes* in me. She no shit does. And that's why she's my ticket out of here. And if you told her all kinds of lies, if she heard bad things about me, stopped believing—that would be kind of hard for me to take. I really don't much want that to happen."

"Corky, listen to the Postman, huh. I listened to you, you listen to me. You gotta let this settle into your cerebellum, kid: you are not, right now, as we sit here, responsible."

"I *am*, though."

"Sorry."

"And that's what you're gonna do, right?—go all around, tell everybody, take out a full-page ad in *Variety*, 'Corky Withers is not as we sit here responsible.'"

"Kid, you've got to let me help—I've got friends, I know people, great doctors—"

"—he means headshrinkers," Fats cut in.

"Shut up," Corky said.

"Kid listen to the Postman!—with your talent comes problems, I know, I've seen a half century easy—I *knew* Houdini—Ehrich Weiss, and he was a card man before he got into the escape racket—but you're a bigger talent—yes—with talent comes problems and Houdini was a fruitcake, believe me—"

"—he just called you crazy—" Fats said.

"—shut up—" Corky said.

"—he said, schmucko, that Houdini was a fruitcake and you were bigger than Houdini which makes you a bigger fruitcake—"

"—he didn't say that, he's on our side—"

"—he's the fucking villain, don't forget that—*never forget that*—"

"I can prove it," the Postman whispered.

"Prove what?" Corky asked.

"That you're not responsible."

"How?"

"Easy. I'll make you a deal. I'll ask you to do a little something that anyone ought to be able to do, and if you can do it, we'll forget the whole thing, and if you can't, we'll think about you seeing somebody fast, is it a deal?"

"Name it," Corky said.

"Make Fats shut up for five minutes," the Postman said.

*   *   *

Corky couldn't help but laugh. "Five *minutes?* I can make him shut up for five years."

"Good. You sit in the chair with Fats and I'll sit here on the couch and we can pass the time."

Corky sat in the chair. "I feel like a jerk if you want to know," he said.

The Postman got out an Individuale.

"Is it okay if *we* talk?" Corky wanted to know. "Or does it have to be like we've locked our mouths and thrown away the key?"

"At your service." The Postman lit his cigar, blew a stream of smoke.

Corky asked, "How long so far?"

The postman looked at his watch. "Thirty-five seconds."

"Gosh," Corky said, "that gives me four minutes and twenty-five seconds to go, think I'll make it?"

The Postman tried to smile.

Corky said, "You don't happen to have another one of those?" He pointed to the cigar.

The Postman handed over the package.

"Take two, they're big," Corky said. He laughed a little. "Remember when you said that?"

"A pro never forgets his good lines," the Postman said.

"How long now?" Corky asked.

The Postman looked at his watch again. "Over a minute."

"Do you think we'll laugh about this someday? If the special works and I get a series, we could give a big article to *TV Guide*."

"Maybe," the Postman said.

Corky said, "I wonder what we'll call it?"

The Postman shrugged.

"How long?" Corky said. "Two minutes yet?"

The Postman shook his head.

Corky smiled, sat back, inhaled deeply on the cigar.

The Postman drummed his fingers.

Silence.

Silence.

Corky smiled again.

The Postman flicked some ashes.

"This is very cruel of you, you know that," Corky said.

The Postman said, "I don't mean it to be."

Corky went on: "I don't know if I'll ever be able to forgive you."

Quietly, the Postman said, "We'll just have to see."

Corky explained, "It's the principle—there's only trust, and once that's gone, what else is there?"

The Postman flicked some more ashes. "Not a whole lot. But we never signed, remember? On account of principle. I got no hold on you, kid. You're free."

"How much longer?" Corky wondered.

The Postman glanced at his watch again. "Two minutes or a little more to go."

Corky closed his eyes. "I can't make it."

The Postman answered softly back: "I didn't think you could."

"Hello everybody, this is Mrs. Norman Maine," Fats said. "My mother thanks you, my father thanks you, my sister thanks you and I thank you," Fats said. "You have nothing to fear but fear itself, nothing to give but blood sweat and tears, nothing ventured nothing gained, nothing to lose but our souls. Here I am boys—here I am world—here's Fats!"

The Postman stood slowly.

"Where the fuck you think you're going?" Fats said. He turned to Corky. "You're not letting him the hell out of here?"

"No more games," the Postman said.

"I think you better sit down," Corky said.

"Kid, I lived through Tallulah Bankhead and the death of vaudeville, I don't scare easy." He stared at the door.

"I'm not gonna let you out of here until you promise not to tell," Corky said.

The Postman started walking.

"I need my chance," Corky said.

"The only chance you got is to get help, kid, and that's what's gonna happen."

Corky grabbed for the old man, spun him back toward the

couch, but the Postman never lost his balance and then he was screaming at Corky, louder than Corky had ever heard from him before, screaming, "Don't you *ever* raise a hand to me again."

Corky sagged.

The Postman resumed his journey to the door.

"You're taking my one chance," Corky pleaded.

"Not taking, giving," the Postman replied, and then he was out the door with Corky standing in the middle of the room, slumped, watching the outside night, and before the door was even shut Fats was on him, going, "He's right, he's goddam right, you're some crazy fuck," and Corky said, "I tried" and Fats shouted, "Tried? *Tried?* You *failed!*"

Corky started pacing while Fats blasted on—"Ever since we got together we knew one thing—one thing—we were *special*— different, sure, to them, to all those pissant drones who make up the western world but not us—and they'll never understand us special ones, they never have, the world'll look level before they ever do—and—and—*Goddammit look at me—*"

Corky stopped the pacing.

"You know it's the hatch for you."

"Maybe not. He only wants to help, you heard—"

"Dream on—"

"There's nothing wrong with me—"

"—I know that and you know that but those pissants, they hate the special ones—they don't know what to do with us—so they hide us—they put us somewhere deep and lonely—and keep us there till they kill us or we die—"

"—don't talk that way—it's not true—"

"I don't understand you anymore—truth is all I'm talking— why does it bother you to hear it, don't you care about anything anymore?—Jesus, don't you even care about the girl?—"

"—Peg?—I love Peg—"

"—well maybe if she really loves you back she'll bring you Crayolas on visiting day and you can color together—" Corky covered his ears. "Oh that's good, that's helpful, that's gonna accomplish a lot—Peg's gonna see it all, gonna see them come for you here and put you in your nice white jacket and cart you off to the hatch and that'll make her feel swell, you'll both have a lot to be proud of, you can face the future great that way, you in your padded cell, her outside trying to mouth words like 'How do you feel this week, Corky? Are they treating you nice, Corky, well I'm glad, Corky because I can't take it anymore, Corky, I'm not coming back to see you ever, Corky, good-bye, good-bye, *good-byeeeeeee.*'"

"What do you *want* from me?"

"—you know—"

"—I don't—"

"—liar—"

"—tell me—"

"—weakling—"

"—I'm not, I'm not, *tell me*—"

"—stop him—"

"—I can't—"

"—stop the Postman—"

"—I tried—"

"—gutless fuck—"

"—I did try—"

"—stop him—"

"—how—"

"—*stop him*—"

"—*How? How? With what?*" and before the words were barely spoken Fats was going *"MEE-MEE-MEE-MEE-MEE—"* and before the Postman was barely halfway up the path the first blow sent him backwards but not down and he looked amazed, managed "Huh?" before Corky swung again, holding Fats by the feet, swinging him like an ax, and this time Fats' heavy wooden head crashed into the Postman's nose and it cracked and now there was blood as the Postman started staggering, tried raising his ancient arms but Fats penetrated the defense as if it wasn't there and this blow started blood from the right eye and the Postman was on his knees now and Fats smashed the top of his bald head this time and now the Postman could only crawl giving Fats a chance at the back of his neck and now they were off the path in the trees and brush and Corky swung again and again and the blood was spraying now but Fats kept crying "A-*gain,* a-*gain*" and each time he connected there was less from the Postman and when there was nothing left from the Postman, nothing at all, Corky dropped the dummy beside the old man and fell to his knees in the underbrush until he could control his tears . . .

Groaning. Intense and continual. Corky jumped up. The night was dark enough so that even though he wasn't far from the Postman, Corky couldn't make him out clearly. He scrambled back.

The Postman lay silent. The sound came from Fats.

". . . Laddie . . . Laddie . . ."

"What?"

". . . my head . . . you broke it . . ."

Corky grabbed Fats, tried to see. It wasn't light enough to see so he put his hands beneath Fats' wig. The skull was starting to splinter.

"What'll I do?"

". . . can't think . . . help me, Laddie . . ."

"I will, I will," and he ran the distance back to the cabin, lay Fats down on the sofa. He stripped Fats naked, carefully took off his wig.

". . . hurry . . ."

"I'm *trying.*"

Corky went to Fats' special fitted case, took out a change of clothes, some extra canvas strips. He ripped the strips into thin pieces, like long shoelaces, deftly bound them around the skull, knotting them tightly until the fit was right. Then he replaced the wig, went back to the case, got out a railroad cap that matched the overalls outfit Fats would now have to wear, pulled it down tight. "Better?" he picked Fats up.

"Oh Christ, I guess so. Does it show?"

"Not with the cap down tight. Let me get you into these other clothes."

"Get off that shirt first. You're blood all over. I don't want to risk getting it on the new clothes."

Corky nodded, tore off the bloody shirt, threw it in the closet, grabbed the sweater Peg had brought down earlier in the evening, pulled it on. Then he went back to Fats, made sure none of his levers had been damaged, began getting him into his clean outfit.

"We'll have to dispose of the body," Fats said.

Corky said "How?"

"I'm not sure yet, I can't think straight yet, but I'll come up with something."

"I know you will, you've got to." He buttoned Fats into his kid's-sized coveralls. "I think maybe the best thing would be to bury him—there's millions of acres of woods around here."

"Oh that's good," Fats said. "That's a humfuckingdinger of a notion—why don't you just amble on up to the house and ask for a shovel—Peg would never think that was a strange request or anything—hell, everybody goes around here digging in the middle of the night."

"Please don't be sarcastic."

"Just go get the goddam Postman and let me do the thinking, all right."

"Anything," Corky said, and he carefully propped Fats back into his overstuffed chair and then ran back out into the dark. It was getting colder, or maybe it had always been and he hadn't noticed it earlier, but even with the sweater on he was shaking terribly. He hurried up the path and moved into the brush where the Postman was, only the Postman was gone . . .

9

When Corky had touched her nipples with his index finger and then gone out the door, at that moment Peg felt, no pun intended, snowed. The barrage of affection he had, no pun intended, laid down, well, it wasn't the kind of thing you listened to every day.

And he meant it.

Didn't he? Peg went into the main room and got the fire going, sat in front of it, stared. Well he would have to be some kind of creature from the black lagoon if he was lying, since the whole point to b.s.ing women was to *get* them to put out and he'd done most of his *after* the deed was done.

Twice.

And I don't even feel guilty, she decided. I feel ter-*rific*. For years she had wondered about the aftereffects of unfaithfulness and to her horror, there weren't any. You could have been doing this for years, she told herself. Would probably have been good for your complexion.

But leave her husband? Leave Duke? For a wandering magician she hadn't seen in fifteen years? People just didn't do things like that.

Why didn't they?

Peg stretched out, watched the wood. They didn't because a bird in the hand you could at least grab hold of and hang on. It was there. What if she decided okay, screw my life, I'll zoom off into the wild blue etc. with Cork and it didn't work out. Sure, he said they'd go off alone, just the two of them, but eventually he'd have to go to work, there'd be agents like that old guy from the afternoon, and workouts with Fats getting their routine honed and tension and maybe he wouldn't make it, it was the iceberg era for magicians nowadays, so she'd end up stranded someplace maybe with a miserable Corky and some slobby dummy staring down from the mantelpiece.

Stay where you are, sister, Peg decided. Maybe you're forlorn, lost, unnoticed, but at least the man selling you tv dinners knows your name. And that means something.

Don't ask what.

She got up and went to the self-help section of her library. There was a time when *The New You* was kind of a bible to her, but that was a while ago, when she was considering going back to college, commuting to Rockland maybe twice a week, but Duke had ridiculed the notion and she had to admit it, he was more than probably right.

The truth was, she decided all on her own, that she was limited. Not such a terrible thing. Better than being bright but cruel. Better than a lot of things.

Limited.

Limited.

She bored people eventually. Or she would if she hung around them long enough. Corky she'd bore too. Oh for now she might make him happy. He dreamed she was fifteen, and when she was fifteen she was, and she knew it, something, and as long as he kept that old image fresh, they'd be fine.

Otherwise, forget it. Forget it, forget leaving, forget it all, keed.

She took down *The New You.*

She went back to the fire and thumbed around until she got to the chapter on men. The particular subsection that came as close as any to her situation was called "Two Is Less Than Half as Much as One," and the point of it was simply that when you were torn you couldn't give yourself to anybody the way The New You wanted to. So what you had to do was make a list and add it up and make a choice. The book was very big on lists. You wrote your problems down, made script of your emotions, so you could judge them better. Lists of ten. And you put the lists side by side to compare. Peg got a large piece of scratch paper and on one half wrote CORKY in capi-

tal letters and on the other, DUKE. Then she scribbled down
qualities. When she was done, she studied her work:

CORKY	DUKE
1) I don't love Corky.	1) I don't love Duke either.
2) I like Corky a lot though. (From what I've seen of him.)	2) Duke's okay.
3) Corky understands me.	3) Duke doesn't give a shit.
4) Corky loves me. (*Says* he loves me.) (Means it?????)	4) Duke doesn't give a shit.
5) Corky and I see things the same way.	5) Duke and I don't talk so much. (Not to each other anyway.)
6) Corky's attractive.	6) Duke doesn't look so much like Elvis anymore.
7) Corky is sweet and nice and kind and gentle.	7) Duke tries.
8) Corky is a good fuck.	8) Duke tries.
9) Corky is a success.	9) Sorry about that, Duke.
10) Corky is *romantic*.	10) Duke couldn't spell "romantic."

She was thumbing through to the List Analysis section
when the phone rang. She got up and answered, knowing it

was Duke, because when he was away on a selling trip or whatever, whenever he was coming home, he always called an hour before he got there, so if he was hungry she could have time to get something heated. "Finast Cabins," she said.

"It's the Duker on the horn."

"Hi honey."

"Be home in 'bout an hour."

"Be waitin'." She could hear the jukebox going in the background. Probably he was with a woman, more than probably he was drinking. Just to hear him lie she asked, "Where you calling from?"

"Your friendly Standard station."

"Sell lots of cutlery?"

"Never doubt the Duker."

"Never have, never will. Hungry for anything special?"

"Thaw me out some chicken, maybe. No, wait—you got any of those ham steak dinners?"

"Better'n that—how would you like a real steak dinner? I bought a couple today."

"Gettin' awful fancy in our old age."

"They were on special and I just wanted to surprise you; you've been working hard enough, you deserve it."

"Aren't you the smart one?" he said, and they hung up.

Peg went back to the List Analysis. Being a new you meant change. But the trick was to know when to do it. Because, the book said, the reason we were unhappy and wanted change was because we made ourselves unhappy on purpose, only we didn't know it, and sometimes we made changes thinking we were making good changes only what we were really doing was making things that much worse, forcing the old you to stick around.

In a list of ten, if it was five-five or six-four, the advice: stay where you are. If it was seven-three: think hard about changing. Anything over seven-three the new you was calling and you had to go. Peg went back over her list, totaling it up.

Duke lost, nine-zero with one even, the first, she didn't love, really love, either of them. My God, Peg realized, nothing's supposed to be that high, the book doesn't even have it listed. If something's that one-sided, you *changed*.

Go with Corky.

Leave with someone you haven't seen for fifteen years and then for less than thirty-six hours.

Run away with someone who loves you.

Go with someone who remembers what you were.

Pray he never sees what you are.

Limited.

And don't you dare *ever* grow old.

More confused than ever, Peg put the book back, got out Johnny Mathis' Greatest Hits, had the record all cleaned and the needle in place before she realized her blunder.

Without even grabbing a coat, she ran out the door. And down along the path toward his cabin, hurrying through the trees, not stopping until she heard Corky crying out, "*No closer,*" and why was he standing off the path in the bushes, sounding that way.

"Corky, listen—"

"—go on back up to the house, please—"

"—Duke called."

"Tell me later, Peg, huh?"

"What's the matter?"

"I'm just trying to get my head on straight, nothing's the matter."

Peg took a step back, away from him.

He moved out onto the path. "I'll come on up in a while."

"We don't have a while."

"What's so goddam important about your husband calling?"

"*I didn't tell him you were here.*"

"So?"

"He's going to know why. The second he gets here and finds out, he's going to catch on—I told him there was steak and he thought *that* was funny, I could tell from what he said, and there's Scotch and French wine and he's going to know what we did, Corky, and I'm afraid."

"You'll get sick, standing around without a coat—get back to the house, it's cold."

"Why are you acting so funny?"

"How am I acting?"

"Why were you wandering around outside if it's so cold?"

"I had some thinking to do."

"About me?"

"No. I swear."

"If it is, say so—we've got to be honest with each other, Corky—I don't like what's happening all of a sudden—I don't know what I'm getting into."

"Hey . . ." He put his arm around her. "Come on. Let me walk you back."

"He's going to know."

"You're just making trouble for yourself."

"I can't hide it. It's going to show all over my face."

"Not if you don't let it."

"You were thinking about me outside, weren't you—you were having second thoughts."

"Not about you."

"Tell me. I never did anything unfaithful before, Corky— I'm not very confident just now—" and then her voice got strident again—"that's *Duke's* sweater. If he sees you in that, he'll know what we did."

Corky started rubbing her shoulders. "If he sees us in bed, he'll have a good chance of knowing; otherwise, it's kind of circumstantial. The way you're going on, if the sun comes up tomorrow, he'll know what we did. If the tides go out, he'll catch on. God forbid the stars should come out."

They were by the front door now. "You think I can lie my way through?"

"You did great with the Postman."

She nodded. "I did, that's right."

"Everything's okay then?"

"You wouldn't feel like maybe coming in for a nightcap or coffee or anything?"

"I don't think it's too smart for me to be up here in case he comes early. My God, if he saw us having Yuban together, he'd be sure to catch onto what we did."

"You making fun?"

"Little maybe."

"Deserved." She looked at him. "But, see, I never acted like a whore before."

"Look on the bright side," Corky told her. "At least you don't feel guilty about it."

Peg started laughing. She moved into his arms and he held her until it came from down in the brush, the terrible scream of the cat. "Don't be frightened, it's just a bird."

Without meaning to shake his head, Corky shook his head: the cat had found the Postman.

10

"Wanna bet?"

Corky blinked. "Bet?"

"You were shaking your head I was wrong when I said it's a bird. I'll betcha I'm right—c'mon, I'll prove it." She took a step down the path.

Corky pulled her to a halt.

Peg looked at him.

"Go inside, Peg."

"What's the matter with you?"

"You want to know the truth, I don't think it's very smart for us to be seen together. I think if he sees us together, we might not be able to pull it off."

"You're scared too then?"

"I'd love for you to show me Sherlock's bird, but I think our cause would be better served if you went inside and did whatever you ordinarily do when your husband comes home."

"Christ," Peg said, "the list. I wrote some things down on a piece of paper, I didn't throw it out yet. It wouldn't be so hot if he saw them."

"I think we both have things we have to do, don't you?"

"I guess."

"Let's do them then." He opened the door for her, she slipped inside, he closed the door.

Then he broke into a wild run down the path, a mistake because he tripped on the goddam roots, fell headlong, didn't care, got up again, ran on. When he reached the area he stopped, looking around, trying to figure out where the cat scream had come from, turned around and around on the path, staring at the woods and brush and then he saw the cat's eyes glowing and he plunged toward them and the night was dark, but when he got there he could see the animal sitting on the Postman who lay facedown and still. Corky looked back to where the assault had been and it was amazing he'd been almost dead, the Postman, but he was like Rasputin, when they tried to kill Rasputin he kept popping back from death on them, almost but not quite taking the final plunge and the Postman had been tough like that too, at his age and with what he'd taken, he'd somehow been able to crawl, what, twenty yards through the thick brush, maybe more.

Corky came close to the body but the cat didn't like that. He kept sitting on the Postman, perched there ready to spring, his claws digging into the back of the Postman's tan overcoat. Corky knelt down and the cat snapped—it was his toy, this body, it belonged to him and he was going to drag it somewhere and devour it like the dark birds—he stared at Corky, eyes insanely bright, hissing, and for a moment Corky wondered if it would be safe to reach for the Postman but when he tried and the cat jumped at his hand, he knew it wasn't so he grabbed blindly for a stick, swung it at the animal, missed, but the cat at least was ten feet away now. Corky grabbed the Postman's feet, dragged him quickly back to the cabin with the cat tracking them all the bloody way.

The blood was going to be a problem and he asked Fats about it once he was back inside.

"You're just going to have to beat everyone else up in the morning," Fats said. "You're rising with the dawn, schmucko, and doing your best to cover up. Need I say your best has only got to be perfect? Where's the Postman now?"

"Just outside—the goddam cat thinks he's a toy."

"Bring me any identification," Fats said so Corky went outside into the dark, took off the Postman's watch, took his wallet and bill clip thick with hundreds and brought them inside, put them on the arm of the overstuffed chair. "Take off your clothes," Fats said then.

"Why?"

"The Postman's going for a swim."

"I can't."

"Not only can you, you're on your way."

"I'm not a strong swimmer," Corky said.

"You're going to have to be strong enough to get him out in the middle before you let him sink."

"I can't do that—see, I'm really not at home in the water—and besides, I know this lake—there's snapping turtles in there —it's true—and there was a water moccasin scare once—"

"I don't care if the Loch Ness Monster's out there and ravenous—"

"—don't talk like that—"

"—hey, hey, Laddie—easy now."

"I don't want to go out in the water—I'm not sure what I want to do but maybe . . ."

"Don't trail your voice off on me. You think I'm going to beg you to tell me what follows your 'maybe.' Well, I'm quite content without knowing, thank you very much."

"Maybe I should give myself up," Corky said then.

Fats made no reply.

"You think?"

"Fine. Do it."

"I'm afraid is the thing."

"You're kind of scared of everything these days, aren't you?"

"I *killed* somebody, for God's sake—I took a life—"

Fats got ministerial. "Dearly Beloved—"

"—the Postman is dead, don't make jokes."

"Why is he dead? Do you remember your logic?"

"He was gonna have me put away."

"And now, what do you think would happen to you if you gave yourself up?"

"They'd put me away, I guess."

"Kee-rect. And since you have just proved conclusively you're not thinking logically, let me take over. Situation: a corpse outside the door. Problem: how to dispose of said object. Now, since corpses tend to sink when given the opportunity, if we had a large enough body of water in the vicinity, we could dip the one into the other and all our troubles would be over. But wait—what is that liquid mass just beyond the cabin edge? It is a large enough body of water. Solution: even to a pointy head like yourself, it should be clear enough."

"I'm really scared, don't you understand that?"

"I'M SCARED TOO—YOU THINK I WANT YOU GOING TO PIECES ON ME. GODDAM YOU. DO WHAT YOU HAVE TO DO."

Corky got undressed down to his shorts, turned, left the cabin. The cat was still by the body but he shooed it away easier this time, picked the Postman up under the arms, dragged him to the edge of Lake Melody. As he got closer, his feet began to sink slightly into the moist sandless shore. The air was terribly cold now, but the water was worse, and Corky stopped for a moment when he was up to his knees and genuinely wondered if he could go on, but since there wasn't any choice, he went on, moving slowly along the mud bottom of the dark lake until he was up to his waist. Then he tried moving the Postman into a lifesaving position, one arm around the body, over the shoulder, curving around the chest, gripping tight under the armpit. Once the grip was secure he pushed off, and slowly, very slowly, began to sidestroke out toward the middle of Lake Melody. The lake was shallow for a good portion of the way, not really getting deep for well over a hundred yards. Corky continued kicking, tried to ignore the incredible cold, tried to figure just how far he would have to go before it was safe to unload his cargo and get back to blessed land. He was probably fifty yards from shore now—he could only guess by the receding light from his cabin—not nearly far enough, and for a moment he thought his left calf was starting to cramp but he moved it very fast several times and the discomfort went away. The Postman was getting heavier and heavier as he stroked slowly along, the tan overcoat sponging up water, and that made it slower, harder, and Corky was starting to labor now, starting to shake terribly from the cold and when the snapping turtle struck at first he was so numb he didn't quite know what was happening, but then when the jaws started pulling at his thigh flesh, when the blood began pouring from the wound—

—stop it—they sleep—they sleep at night and there aren't any after you, don't think—

Corky kept his mind blank, and when the turtles bunched for an attack he thought them away and kept on and when the fangs of the water moccasin dug into his neck, he thought that away too, just kept on and on and nothing frightened him at all until he realized that in the middle of the murky lake surrounded by darkness and cold he was no longer the only one alive, there wasn't any doubt, and he wasn't going crazy, the Postman was breathing and Corky screamed, and the cry skimmed along the slick surface and he dropped his bundle and was about to start for shore except the Postman would not let go—the old man would not die and he would not let go, his thin fingers held to Corky's wrist and Corky struck out with his free hand but no good, *the old man was indestructible* and now they were facing each other and the Postman's eyes were open and blinking slowly like a withered crocodile's and now his hands were moving up Corky's body and when the thin fingers reached his neck they locked on tight and Corky pounded but the Postman was beyond pain, and as his fingers continued to constrict around Corky's neck he realized omigod, omigod, *he's* trying to kill *me* and they sank below the dark surface then, Corky trying to grip the old man's fingers, trying to break them like stiff twigs from his jugular but they would not loosen, they held, they held, and Corky hadn't gotten a decent breath, the surprise had taken him too quickly and he could feel his heart already trying to break from his chest and his temple was pounding too and the old man held, held, he had been alive a million years and he had no intention of going quickly or quietly or at all and Corky began to think he was about to drown and he fought hard and somehow kicked briefly to the surface and they thrashed awhile for air and then down again, and Corky, rejuvenated, reached out his hands and grabbed the Ancient's and as they sank deeper and deeper into the lake center he began to get leverage and then he had one hand loose and then the other and my God he'd done it, he was safe, safe, he'd won and he kicked to the surface, panting but alive and that was the object of it all wasn't it, staying alive, and he treaded water before he realized that somewhere in this chilled darkness the Postman was alive and swimming more than likely for shore but where—where—and Corky tried listening but he couldn't hear because he was panting too terribly and he turned around in the water, around and around, and this time he really did feel something around his legs, but it didn't matter, there wasn't time to fill your mind with wildness now, now there was an old man to find in a dark sea and Corky realized that what had been around his legs had been his muscles starting to surrender to the cold, cramping, and if they got bad enough, good-bye, but until that happened he had to keep looking, keep looking, and now his stomach was starting to tighten slightly and that would have been funny, getting murdered by a corpse, some epitaph, except he wasn't going to get murdered and the Postman wasn't a corpse, yet, and Corky turned in the water, turned and spun and there he was, at last, the Postman, swimming feebly for shore, and oh, Corky thought as he covered the distance between them, oh oh oh, he thought as he overtook the Ancient, pushed and held him down till death and after, and as at last the Postman sank at last forever, Corky could only shake his head in awe at the things we do for love . . .

11

"There's breakfast anytime you want it," Peg said.

Corky stood in the doorway of the cabin. "What's wrong?" The morning was chill.

"Just make believe everything's fine—Duke's watching us from the house I think."

"Why?"

"Because what I said would happen happened—we had a steamer last night—'Why didn't you tell me someone was here? You lied, why did you lie?' I said I didn't I only forgot. I didn't tell him anything about yesterday. Not word one."

"You think he wants me up there now?"

"I think he wants to watch us together."

"Give me five minutes, I'll be there, can he read lips?"

Peggy shook her head confused.

"Then I'd like to say thank you for the invitation, and I adore you, and I appreciate the opportunity of having breakfast, and fucking you was just maybe the experience of my lifetime, and I take my coffee black, and your breasts belong in the Louvre which is a museum in Paris which is a place I would love to visit with you once you decide to leave that suspicious asshole up in the house."

"Are you ever something," Peg said, careful to stop smiling before she turned, faced the house, headed up.

Corky hurried inside, started shaving. "Getting very suave with the words there," Fats said. "Urfuckingbane."

"Praise from Caesar." Corky glided his razor down along his cheeks. "Wanna come along?"

"I got nothing else on the agenda. Besides, I wanna see what the old ear-blower looks like."

Corky was rocked by the change. The Ronnie Wayne who had him take his notes across the library, the senior with the convertible and the Elvis hairdo; not a remnant left. The one sipping coffee at the kitchen table was almost completely bald, beer-bellied, with the puffiness under the eyes that only an excess of alcohol supplies.

"My God Ronnie how are you," Corky said, crossing the floor with Fats, right hand out.

"The Duker's doing okay," and he stood, and they shook, then they sat.

"You take your coffee—" Peggy began, about to say "black," but the quick turn of Duke's head warned her, and she ended with the word "how?" which was fine.

"Nothing," Corky answered, and she nodded, poured him a cup.

"Sorry I wasn't here to greet you yesterday. Help with the entertaining and all. But somebody's got to earn a living, I guess."

"You're still in real estate, isn't that right?" Corky asked.

"I gave that up," Duke said. "Dull. Who needed all that bullshit, the goddam pressure all the time when what I really love is just to fish and hunt, take your pick. When I want to think, I just go out on the lake here and cast a plug around and let my mind clean out."

"He fishes every chance he gets, God knows," Peggy said.

Duke looked at her. "I'm out of real estate awhile now. Just doing a little selling nowadays. Surprised Peg didn't bring you up to date."

"She may have, the truth is, I was so whipped when I got here she fed me and the wine hit me fast which I should know by now it always does."

"Corky's a lot of fun when he's bombed," Fats cut in. "He spends half his time trying to be witty—you might call him a half-wit."

Corky looked at Fats. "You can do better than that."

Fats looked right back at him. "Why bother, you'd miss the punch lines." He turned to Duke. "Corky here is afflicted with diarrhea of the mouth and constipation of the brain, very rare."

"I'd just like to drink my coffee in peace, do you mind?" Corky said.

"He's that dumb?" Duke asked.

Fats answered, "Dumb? If it started raining soup and we all quick ran outside to eat, Corky would be the one carrying a fork."

Duke began to laugh.

"Don't encourage him," Corky said.

"Clever," Duke said to Corky. "It really is."

"Don't tell *him* that, tell *me* that," Fats said. "I'm the talent."

"My mistake," Duke said.

"So what are you selling," Fats wanted to know. "I'm in the market for a penis, my last one caught Dutch elm disease, it's murder getting an erection."

Both Duke and Peggy went on that one.

Corky sighed. "No one is interested, I assure you."

"Corky," Fats said, "you just don't understand—surely someone of your acquaintance must have had an erection sometime, ask them about it."

"Back to the lumberyard with you, I mean it."

"Tell us about your sex life, Corky, we all love short stories."

Corky put his hand over Fats' mouth and asked, "What kind of selling do you do exactly?" while at the same time, Fats was going "Mmm-mmm-mmm."

Duke just shook his head. "My God, how do you do that? Your lips don't move or anything. You're terrific, you are. I'm really glad you're here for me to see."

"Thank you," Corky said. He looked down at Fats. "Will you be good now?"

Fats nodded.

"I mean it; promise?"

Fats nodded harder.

Corky took his hand away.

Fats whispered, "Ask him if he's glad that I'm here too."

Duke smiled. "The both of you," he answered back. And after that, whatever tension there might have been at the beginning was gone, and it turned out Duke sold kitchen items to housewives, mostly door-to-door, he liked personal contact work was why, and he had a terrific line of only top quality merchandise, everything from can openers to cutlery, and he also sidelined in baby things, an addition he had thought of because a lot of young mothers had trouble finding time to get to the store, and Fats got excited about the baby clothes, since he was running short of underwear and asked what the largest size Duke sold was and Duke said I'll give you a dozen pairs free so Fats said how about throwing in some cutlery, Corky's a great whittler and Duke said sure, why not, but Corky insisted that whatever he took he was going to pay for and Duke said let me get my line, pick what you want and he hurried upstairs where his suitcases were.

"How'd I do?" Corky whispered when it was safe.

"Just unbelievable," she whispered back.

"Too bad Fats wasn't here," Fats said, hurt in his tone; "Fats might have been a little help now and then getting the old conversational ball going."

"You're *always* unbelievable," Peggy said.

"Brains as well as boobs." Fats turned to Corky. "No wonder you love her."

"Shhhh," Peggy said.

But she was smiling.

Duke came back with his merchandise and Fats was crushed because none of the baby stuff would fit him but Corky liked the cutlery and Fats insulted Corky a few times about things in general, and they talked some about selling techniques and Duke explained where the skill came but in spite of his success with it, enough was enough, the main thing was to close up the cabins and get the house in the best order possible and just sell the whole place, property and all and move on, so while Corky finished his second cup of coffee and Peg set to work tidying the kitchen Duke excused himself, put on his Windbreaker and went outside to work on the grounds awhile, and when they were safely alone again Corky applied a little pressure on Peg to get out, but not in any pushy way, and she responded gently, explained she was really confused, really trying to get *her* head on straight now, and they talked quietly, nothing much of import happening at all, until Duke came in a little while later with the news that he'd found the Postman's Rolls-Royce in the woods.

12

He didn't know it was the Postman's of course. He was sure it was a Rolls though. "Strangest thing," Duke said. "I thought I was losing my mind. There I was, walking along, trying to figure out which I should do this aft, go hunting or stay around here and fish, and I'm nearing the back road—"

"—where's that?" Corky wondered.

Duke pointed out past the cabins. "It's not even much of a road. It's just kind of a rutty path that leads along the edge of the property. Down out of sight from the main drag you take to get here. And then I saw this thing. And I thought, son of a bitch, what is that, that looks like a goddam Rolls-Royce but that's ridiculous, only when I got closer, it wasn't so ridiculous, because there it was bigger'n life. Somebody took that stupid rutty back road into here and got stuck—it's muddy as hell—and left it. *Left it.*"

"I wonder who it could be," Peggy said.

"Shouldn't take me long to find out," Duke told her. "If it was a Ford or something, yeah, but a white Rolls—"

"—*white* did you say?" Corky cut in, and now his voice sounded excited.

"White. Off-white—around in there—"

"—was it a Corniche?"

"—what's that—?"

"—*did the top come down?*"

Duke nodded.

"Show me!" Corky said and he took off out the door, Duke behind him.

"That's gotta be the Postman's," Corky said when they got there. He walked around the car. It was sideways on the almost invisible road, and the front wheels were stuck in deep mud. "Why would he leave it though?" He looked at Duke. "A car like this must cost over fifty thousand. I know he's rich —he smokes nothing but four-dollar cigars—but this is ridiculous. I hope nothing's the matter with him."

"Can you find out?"

"Goddam right I can and I'm gonna." He pointed to the car. "Can you get it unstuck without hurting it?"

"I'd sure love to try," Duke said. "I never even sat in a fifty-thousand-dollar car, much less drove one."

"Don't force it, huh?"

"I won't, Corky. I know cars pretty good. You can trust me."

"Be back in a couple minutes," Corky said, and he started running again.

Peggy was waiting in the kitchen when he got there. "I've got to call New York right away, is that all right? That may be the Postman's car and I've got to check that he's okay."

"Where's Duke?"

"Getting it unstuck."

"Did he say anything about me or anything?"

"Not now, huh darling? This could be kind of important. Living room phone okay?"

She nodded, stayed in the kitchen. She had the broom out and was starting to sweep the place when she heard Corky. She swept a little more.

"Sadie it's me, let me speak to the boss."

Pause.

"I know he's worried about me, tell him to worry about the stock market. I just got a tip IBM's about to go into receivership. Tell him that, it'll give him cardiac arrest. Now would you put him on?"

Pause.

Peg went over and poured herself a speck more coffee.

"Never mind where I am, I'm peachy, you're the one's causing all the trouble, you okay?"

Pause. Then, louder:

"Don't come on to me like that, Postman—I don't need your

views on *my* erratic behavior, my behavior's just fine, thank you—"

Pause. Very loud now.

"So what if I ran away, running away's good for the soul, read the Bible, Postman, and if you want to know what I think, *you're* the one with the erratic behavior mister, at least I'm not senile, at least I'm not leaving fifty-thousand-dollar cars all the hell over in the goddam woods—"

Short pause.

"Forgive me for insulting you, I didn't know it was an eighty-thousand-dollar car."

Now a long pause. Very long.

"What do you mean how do I know where your car is, I know because . . . because . . ."

Quietly now.

"Yeah. Yessir, that's right. I'm at that place, I've been here all the time. Boy am I smart, here I call you to find out how *you* are and you make me slip and tell you where *I* am."

Pause.

"No, I'm not coming back, not yet, not till I get my head really on straight once and for all. When it is, I'll be there, you can count on that."

Loud.

"Don't even think about coming for me—I'm staying."

Soft.

". . . because . . . because . . ."

Whispered.

". . . there's this girl . . ."

Peg moved across the kitchen to the sink and poured out her coffee, washed the cup, put it upside down to drain. She picked up a washcloth next, fiddled with it, then couldn't help herself, got quickly back to the near door, out of sight.

". . . quit saying it's ridiculous, I told you, it's not some moonstruck thing like I just met her, Postman, I went to school with her—I don't care what you say, it isn't crazy—yeah, she's the one you talked to yesterday, the one that told you I might be in Binghamton, I was listening right behind the door."

Peg couldn't help but smile.

". . . I know she's beautiful, she always has been . . . I think she likes me, yeah, she was glad to see me, I'm positive of that."

Long pause.

"No, she isn't married, never was."

Laugh.

"You've got some fantastic memory for an old fart, I forgot she told you she had a husband. It's not a good marriage though, I swear. I'm not breaking up anything that wasn't in trouble to begin with. I'm not a home wrecker, I'm just a guy with his fingers crossed, I got hopes, and I don't want to talk about her anymore just now, I haven't got that much privacy."

Peg went quickly back to the broom, busied herself with getting the floor done, got the dustpan, swept it full, emptied it all into the wastebasket. She had her back to Corky when he came in a little later. He put his arms around her, gently raised his fingers till they cupped her breasts. "We got troubles, baby," Corky said then. "I goofed on the phone call—I let slip where I was."

"You mean he's coming back?"

"I got him to promise not to at the end."

"Well then."

"He's not a patient man, Peg. The Postman gets his way. He's just as liable to limo on up here as not so what I'm saying is I don't want to put on any pressure but there's more pressure now, you've got to make up your mind about leaving."

"I will. Soon."

"Today?"

She nodded.

Corky kissed her. "I think you better come along when I explain about the car to Duke. I'm gonna have to start lying and I need all the help I can get. I don't want Duke knowing you told the Postman I wasn't here. With his suspicious nature, that doesn't help our cause a lot. Cross your fingers."

She kissed him gently. "You are a terrible liar. It all shows in your face."

"There you go, insulting me again."

Duke was waiting when they got there. "Got her out easy," he said, pointing to the car. "Wasn't stuck bad at all. Just started her rocking and out she came."

"I shouldn't have let you do it," Corky said. "It's my fault." "Why?"

"'Cause the Postman happens to be hysterical about his goddam Corniche. He yelled at me for saying it only cost fifty, it was eighty on the hoof."

Duke could only shake his head and mutter, "Eighty, Jesus." He turned to Corky then. "Why'd he leave it behind?"

"Because like I told you, he's richer than Croesus and he's probably got it insured to the teeth, it's no more than if you or me abandoned a flexible flyer."

Duke studied Corky for a while, waiting.

"If I tell you something can I ask you not to nose it around?"

"I guess."

"I'm in hiding. I've got a lot of career problems and I'm not behaving all that normal. I took off when the Postman was coming to my place to pressure me—"

"—what is this Postman name?"

"It's just what he's called in the business. Ben Greene. 'Gangrene' Fats calls him, drives him batty."

"Go on."

"What he just told me was this: he came up here looking to go to Grossinger's—I've been doing a lot of talking about coming back to my beginnings lately—my dad gave massages at the G."

"Oh that's right, sure."

"Well, the Postman took a shot that I'd be at Grossinger's so he tooled on up in his chariot here, only when he passed this place, he said he remembered it but he'd gone by the main entrance and he spotted the back road here and took it."

"Whoa—why in the world would he remember this place?"

"I talk about it all the time, Ronnie. I gave my very first magic show here. In the basement. Peg's kid brother's eighth birthday. It was where it all started."

"I'd forgotten that," Peg said.

"I hadn't," Corky said, "not a bit of it. You saved me. Your brat brother farted and no one was watching my act and you came up with some nutty threat—"

Peg got all excited. *"We were gonna glue his tongue."*

"That's *it*," Corky cried. "Scared him into shutting up. I still remember the tricks I did."

"Hey hold it, huh?" Duke walked over to Corky. "If he came here looking for you, why didn't he find you?"

"It must have been when Peg drove me into town—I told you I got out of New York in a helluva hurry—I needed stuff, toothpaste, toothbrush, that kind of thing."

"You're still not telling me why the goddam car's here!"

Corky smiled. "The Postman didn't plan on leaving it, obviously. He snooped around, decided this place was shut, came back, got in the Rolls, found out he was stuck. So what the hell else was there to do but what he did—walk up to the road, get a ride to the G and call the Rolls people in Manhattan. I just told him I thought he was crazy, let some Exxon jerk do it and he almost came through the phone wires at me: *'Nobody touches my Rolls but a Rolls man!'* He told them to come get him and they said it was a little late, they'd be up tomorrow." Corky looked at his watch. "They should be here within a couple hours. Anyway, the Postman wasn't about to be caught dead in a tacky place like Grossinger's—he's what you might call snobby, as you can kind of guess by what he drives—and he hired one of their limos to get him back to town."

Duke looked at the car awhile.

"Frankly, I think the whole story's crazy," Corky said.

"Well," Peg told him; "it makes perfect sense to me."

Corky looked at Duke and shook his head. "Women," Corky said.

"You must be getting hungry, let me fix some lunch," Peggy said.

Duke said nothing, sipped his Scotch. They were alone in the house now, in the living room, and Duke would not stop pacing.

"What difference does it make for God's sake? So a car's here, who cares?"

"There's something crazy and I think you know what it is, and I care."

"Oh Jesus, I'm sick of that record."

Duke finished his drink, poured himself another.

"That's smart," Peggy said.

"What's the matter, you bought it with money I earned, or is it reserved only for the rich and special guests around here?"

"Go ahead, get drunk, if I'm lucky you'll pass out, at least then it'd be quiet."

"He's really tricky—at breakfast all that shit with the dummy, I really believed it. But now with the car, I'm not buying nothing anymore. People do *not* leave eighty-thousand-dollar cars lying around, I don't care what anybody tells me."

"Well what, then?"

"Maybe it isn't this Postman's car. Maybe it's his. Maybe he's hiding it there just waiting for the chance to take off with my wife."

"Good thinking. Really using the old bean. I hope you noticed I didn't even bother getting mad at your crack about me going off into the sunset. We had enough of that kind of talk already."

"Why goddammit, there's gotta be some explanation—"

"—there is and you've had it—"

"—bullshit—"

"—oh bullshit yourself—"

"—don't wise off back to me—"

"—I'm over twenty-one I'll do what I damn please—"

"—why didn't he get the car out of the mud, I did, it wasn't that hard answer me that goddammit—"

"—maybe he tried, maybe he couldn't, he's old, maybe he was a rotten driver—"

"—old?—"

"—that's right—"

"—how do you know he was old, Corky never said he was old—"

"—last night he did—we were talking about why he came up here and he said this agent was pressuring him and he said how old he was—"

"—you told me you never talked about anything and he said the same—you didn't even tell him I changed jobs and wasn't in real estate anymore—you fed him and he went to bed *now what happened last night?*"

"I won't go through this again."

"Did this Postman stop by? Did you see him? That's how you knew he was old, wasn't it?"

"Goddammit no!"

"Was this before or after you fucked for Corky—"

"—you stop this Duke—"

"—before or after or was it during, did you invite the old guy in to watch?" He put his drink down then and slapped her in the face.

Peg tried running.

No chance. Duke slapped her again. "Did you fuck him, you did, you did goddam it, didn't you?"

"*No!*"

"I'm gonna pound the crap outta you till we get to the truth, did you fuck him?"

"No."

He backhanded her. "*Did you fuck him?*"

"No—Jesus—"

"Did—you—fuck—him?"

"NO BUT I WANTED TO."

He pushed her down into a chair then. "Okay," he said quieter now. "At least we know the truth."

Peggy was crying.

"Those don't work with me, dry the baby blues, don't cut no ice with the Duker." He sipped his Scotch. "I'd like to check out his cabin I can tell you."

". . . why . . ."

Duke shrugged. "Might be interesting, that's all. Might clear up the car thing and who knows, if you *wanted* to fuck him, maybe you *will* when my back's turned—who knows, it would sure save a lot of time if you had everything nice and ready, a nightie hanging in the closet, your diaphragm handy by the bed. That way you could just zip on down there and rip off a little something whenever your nice pure little heart desired."

Peggy dried her eyes and stood. "I'm going out."

"Down to the cabin, pay a little visit to the star?"

"No," Peggy said, and her voice was dry and brittle. "I'm going to town, I'll shop and then I'm going to drive for a long long time. Hours. I've got some decisions to make." She looked at her husband for a while. "Except maybe you've made them for me . . ."

"C'mon," Duke said; "it'll be fun." He stood outside the open door to Corky's cabin and gestured to the rowboat he'd brought to the edge of the lake and the fishing poles and tackle resting inside.

"I'm not crazy about fishing," Corky said from the doorway.

"You can row then, it'll be nice and quiet and we can talk. I just had a good talk with Peg and now I'd like one with you. I told you how fishing just cleans out my mind—who knows maybe it'll do the same for you."

"Where is she?"

"In town. Making a 'decision,' she said."

"You seem upset, Ronnie."

"Why should I be. Surrounded by a good wife, old friends. Peg and I did some talking about you. Might be interesting if we did some talking about her."

"I'll just get a jacket," Corky said, and he quickly went inside. Duke moved into the doorway, started looking around but Corky was back right away. "Let's go."

They went outside. Corky stopped. Duke watched him. "What are you locking the door for? Ain't nobody here but us chickens."

"Habit," Corky said.

"I could take that as an indication that you don't trust me. I don't, of course. We trust each other, don't we?"

"Sure," Corky said.

"Make certain it's really locked up tight and everything," Duke said. "Give it a good shake to be positive."

"I don't have to do that."

"Let me then." He rattled the door hard. "Safe as a baby," he said and they started for the boat. Duke held it for Corky, then got in himself, gave it a shove and they started drifting out toward where Corky had gone swimming.

"Let's row over that way," Corky said. "Give me the oars, I'll do it."

"I know the best fishing spots," Duke explained. "When I get us to the vicinity, you can take over."

"Fine," Corky said. He looked into the water. It was not clear more than a foot or so down.

"What are you looking for?" Duke wondered.

Corky jerked his head up. "Nothing."

"You were sure examining the water awful close."

"Habit. I like staring down, see what I can see."

"You're full of habits, aren't you?" He brought out the bottle of Scotch. It was almost empty now. He offered it to Corky who shook his head. "It was bought for you special. I don't get Scotch."

"I'm not much of a drinker, I told you that." He was staring down at the water again. They were getting very close now.

Duke put the oars up, picked up a rod, opened the tackle box for a plug. "Peggy told me you fucked her last night."

Corky smiled. "Bullshit."

"She went into detail."

"Did she tell you how we smashed the champagne glasses into the fireplace? We thought that was pretty romantic at the time."

Duke weighted his plug, cast it out, let it sink, started reeling in slowly.

"Is that—"

"—shit," Duke cut in. "Snagged on something."

"Is that why you brought me out here? To try and trick me into admitting something that never happened? 'Cause if it is, I'd like to go back in now."

"Heavy," Duke said, pulling with his rod.

"I'd like to go back in now, Duke."

"That's got it," Duke said, and he reeled in his line. He looked at Corky then, cast again, reeled. "What she said was she wanted to go to bed with you. I made her say that. I acted like a fucking animal and she—" He stopped, trying for words. "I'm afraid I'm gonna lose her and I don't want that to happen."

"Come on," Corky said. "Get hold of yourself. You've got to stop going around accusing people, Duke. My God, you gave me just about the happiest times I had in this town. You don't even remember but I was this nothing and you were everything and a couple of times you took me along for fries at The Hut and I sat there with you and Peggy and I thought, I'll never forget this, and I haven't."

Duke shook his head, kept on fishing. "I don't remember any of that, you're right."

"Sure I had a crush on Peggy, my God, everybody had a crush on Peggy. I wasn't even jealous when she started dating you, it was fitting. Shit, I remember carrying notes between you two during study hall and I felt so goddam *proud*. That someone like you would see fit to even use me as a go-between. That was a moment for me."

"It hasn't gone so good for me since then," Duke muttered.

Oh Jesus, Corky thought, I'm trying to steal your wife, don't go getting human on me please . . .

"I fuck around a lot. I'm not proud of it. I just hate it; when I touch Peggy all I feel is I don't deserve her so I take anything I can get from anybody I can get it from."

"Tomorrow you're not gonna be happy you got into this so let's bag it, don't you think?"

"It's important you know. See, that period when you tagged along, that was kind of the high point for me. I never finished college, I wasn't the greatest thing to hit the real estate business, I hate the goddam selling door-to-door. But Peggy, she came in at the top and she's stuck with me all the way, and I'm afraid that if I lose her now . . . well what is there?" He said "Shit," then and tried to get his plug loose but it was stuck again.

"It's cold," Corky said. "Let's go in and build a fire or something."

"I can't get it loose," Duke said. He pulled and pulled. "Christ it's like a whale."

Corky picked up the oars, put them in the water.

"Don't do that, you'll break my pole."

"Just trying to help."

"Well don't help, it's coming, I'm getting the whole thing up now." He put his pole down and took hold of the strong line, pulling it hand over hand.

Corky stared down through the water because something was beginning to become visible.

Hand over hand Duke kept at it.

Corky leaned far over, continued staring down.

"Fuckin' logs," Duke said, grabbing his plug, pulling the hook from the log, letting the log sink back down into the dark water.

Corky cleared his throat and asked, "Anything left in that Scotch bottle?"

Duke handed it over. "You look like you could use it."

"Freezing my nuts off," Corky said, and he drank, waited, drank again. "Okay if we go in now?"

Duke nodded. "I've said my piece," and he took the oars, and they were well on their way back to shore when Duke spotted what looked like a body, half in water, half on land, not all that far away.

13

Corky looked down at the tiny bald man. "I wonder who it can be?"

Duke knelt by the body, turned him over. "I was thinking it might be your Rolls guy."

"You kidding?" Corky said. "The Postman's only about six-foot-three. See what his wallet says."

Duke went into various pockets. "Nothing. Stripped clean."

"Doesn't make sense, there must be something, be sure before—"

"—Christomighty," Duke cut in, "I think he's still alive—"

"—fantastic—"

"—it's just a wild chance but it's worth a whack—can you do artificial respiration?—"

"—don't think so—"

"—all right, goddammit, *I'll* do it, get up to the house, call Normandy Hospital, tell them to haul ass over—"

"—right—"

"—*and stay at the house till they get there so you can bring them straight here*—"

"—gotcha," Corky said, and he got in the boat, got right out again, said "Faster if I run" and took off around the lake going like crazy.

Duke straightened out the body, tilted the head back, opened the mouth. He checked to see that the tongue was all right and it was, not swallowed. Then he glanced at the teeth to see they weren't dentures. Finally he put his fingers together, pinched the old man's nose shut, tilted back his head and blew hard down his throat. He blew a second time. Then a third.

The heart cavity was swelling.

Duke bent down, pressed his head against the aged chest, tried to catch a beat. Nothing. He knelt over the old man then, started pressing very hard on his heart, every second a press, not enough to crack the rib cage, but damn near.

He bent down after a minute of that and listened again.

Nothing.

He started regular mouth-to-mouth resuscitation after that, trying to do it twelve times a minute. Breathe, two, three, four, five, six; breathe, two, three, four, five, six. He kept that up for several minutes.

Still nothing.

He'd been wrong; the old man was dead. Still, as he stood and loaded the corpse into the boat, he felt better for the try. He lowered the body gently down, began rowing across the lake.

Toward Corky's cabin.

Because there was just no doubt in his mind, this one he was ferrying now had to be the owner of the Rolls. It didn't make sense any other way and there had been a tone in Corky's six-foot-three line that rang false. Or maybe it had come too quick. Or maybe any number of things.

Whatever the case, Duke wasn't buying.

He was careful when he drew close to shore to keep Corky's cabin as much as possible between himself and the main house, trying to keep the chances of Corky spotting him as low as possible. He glided the last yards, pulled the rowboat up less than twenty feet from the cabin.

Then he got out, reached into his pocket for his master key, and moved quietly to the locked front door. He had trouble getting it to fit, his hands were trembling, which was the first time he realized he was afraid. He didn't really know what of, didn't know, for that matter, what the Christ he could find in the cabin that would prove much of anything.

But it was worth the whack.

Corky was lying, about something or everything or in-between, and wouldn't it be nice to let old Peg know that kind of info. Peg hated liars, always had, and Duke wanted to be first to spread the news.

He got the door open, stepped fast inside, shut it just as quickly, and the place was darker than he figured, blinds drawn and all, and he waited a moment by the door, relocking it, getting accustomed to the dimness.

He was several steps into the cabin before he cried half aloud, because the goddam dummy was sitting there, watching the door, sitting in a chair by the little kitchenette area and it seemed, for the moment, human, with its staring eyes.

Duke took a breath, got down to business. There were four places he had to look. The bedroom closet, the living room closet, the desk out here and the dresser in there. The living room closet was closest, so that's where he began. Not much really. Corky's clothes on hangers and not many of them. Two suitcases. He opened the first. Empty. Put it back. He opened the second. It was full of dummy crap. A lot of long canvas tapes and changes of clothes.

It scared him again.

There was something fucking loony tunes about walking around carrying kid-sized coveralls for a piece of wood. Probably Edgar Bergen felt like an asshole whenever he went traveling, because he didn't just have Charley, there was the hick, Mortimer Snerd.

Duke closed the closet door, started on the desk. Nothing, nothing nothing. Not a goddam shred.

Shit.

The kitchenette was between the bedroom and living room and he moved past Fats quicker than he had to, because the dummy was voodooing him, no question about it.

The bedroom wasn't quite as dark. He went to the closet but it didn't have anything at all so that left the dresser and if that had nothing, he could always give a glance at the bathroom and the kitchenette maybe—

—but the dresser had everything.

In the top drawer, under some shirts. Duke flicked them over to one side and the first thing he saw was the watch. He brought it close. "Patek Philippe" it read, and he didn't know if it kept decent time or not but it sure as hell looked expensive.

Next to the shirt was a bill clip. Duke sat on the bed staring at it. He pulled the money loose and started counting the hundred-dollar bills.

Three thousand dollars!

Duke just sat there. It was incredible, there were actually people in this world who walked around with that kind of bread in their pockets.

Could it be Corky's? What kind of money did you make when you did guest shots on the tube? Plenty, probably, but *this* much?

Maybe. Duke wasn't sure.

The wallet was what made up his mind. It was in the next drawer down, deep in the corner. Fat. Duke opened it and looked at the credit cards. American Express. Diner's Club. A dozen more. All made out to Mr. Ben Greene.

Duke closed his eyes. What the fuck was this Postman's name. Was it Ben Greene? He couldn't remember.

"Gangrene," Duke said out loud. It *was* the Postman. Corky had told that out by the Rolls, how the dummy called the Postman that, gangrene.

Now he started studying the photographs.

A dozen of them, snapshots all of two people, one of them always famous, the second one always the same. The same little bald guy with Bing Crosby. With Berle. With Sinatra and Hope and it was the same little bald guy who was dead out there now in the rowboat.

It was the Postman. And he wasn't six-foot-three. But Corky lied. Wait, just wait till little old Peg got the news. Maybe at dinner. They'd all be sitting around and he'd bring out the evidence one by one, the watch—and then the bill clip and then—

—wait a minute, why bother with the bill clip, that would be great, he'd keep that out, and if Corky asked for it, he'd be proving himself guilty and if he didn't ask for it, well, the Postman didn't need the three thousand anymore now, did he.

Duke stood up, stuck the watch and wallet in one trouser

pocket, the bill clip and the money safely in his shirt pocket, one that buttoned, and started out of the bedroom in a hurry now—

—and then Fats raised his hand—

—Duke screamed, frozen by the kitchenette curtain because it was moving now and the hand had a knife in it and Fats struck straight ahead, stomach level, and the knife slid in easily above Duke's belt and now the curtain was moving again and here came Fats' other hand and it had its own knife and it curved into Duke's side and Duke bent double and Fats' first knife jammed into the shoulder and the second hand, the left, caught the neck and now Duke was screaming but Fats kept on, right left right left, like a kid's toy beating a brass drum, only those weren't drumsticks, they were knives, and they kept slashing and hitting and Duke thought I'm going blind, I'm going blind but he was wrong, it wasn't that, there was just too much blood in his eyes for him to see . . .

Corky stepped out from behind the curtain, stared numbly down at the corpse.

"Take these goddam things," Fats said and Corky took the knives carefully, laid them in the sink. "The guy was right, he sold top quality merchandise," Fats said.

Corky blinked.

"Those were his knives, schmucko, get with it."

Corky ran to the door, unlocked it, looked out. "What am I gonna do," he said, "Christ, I got the Postman out there and now the other guy and what if Peggy comes home?"

"I'll tell you just what you're gonna do you—"

"—maybe I should get the Rolls—I could fit them in the trunk and—"

"—goddammit listen to me—you go right into my suitcase and you take some pieces of that canvas tape and you take these two and you stick 'em in the boat and you put a rock from outside on their legs and tape 'em there and row right out and over the side they go and if you're not back in fifteen minutes you're a bigger nincomfuckingpoop than even I give you credit for—"

Corky was back in twelve.

He leaned against the inside of the door, closed his eyes. "They dropped like they were being pulled."

"Did you tie a rock to each of them?"

Corky managed a nod.

"Nuts," Fats said; "now I can't say 'two birds with one stone.'"

"Stop with your goddam jokes for once!"

"I'll be glad to if you'll quit standing around with that faraway sensitive look plastered on your face, I got to shock you to get any activity—you're not doing what's got to be done, get to work on this place, clean the knives, get some towels and wash away this blood, you want Peggy to walk in and find out what a sloppy housekeeper you are, *move.*"

She didn't walk in. She called rather, standing on the path halfway down. It was over an hour later and Corky had finished showering. He hurried up to her. It was cold and getting dark and she looked tired.

"You've been through a lot," he said.

She shrugged. "Whatever. Where's Duke?"

"We had kind of a scene. I guess you told him you were interested in me. He wants me outta here. He went hunting. He said he was going to take his time but I got the impression he didn't much want me here when he got back."

Peg nodded.

"Are *you* going to be here when he gets back?" Corky asked. "Or are you coming with me?"

"That's what I wanted to talk about," she said, and turned, led him up into the house where they sat across from each other by the fireplace.

"Okay," Corky said. "Who wins? What's the answer? I don't want you to think I'm pressuring you because I'm not really, the fact that I'll kill myself if you pick him shouldn't enter into your thoughts one way or the other."

She smiled. "You're really wonderful, y'know that?"

"I feel my chances just went up a notch."

"Well you must be *something* pretty special, because we've been together for a fat forty-eight hours after a little absence of fifteen years and we weren't exactly intimate then, and you get me to lie for you and sleep with you and the most incredible thing of all, you got me, today, to *thinking,* which I have been avoiding with ease for most of my natural life."

"I think I just lost the notch," Corky said.

"You gotta try and understand my decision, Cork, 'cause it didn't come easy. I've drunk more coffee in more luncheonettes and driven more miles and argued with myself and screamed out loud in the car—true—and let me get to it."

Corky nodded.

"Okay. Duke: married all these years, not the best advertisement for the tradition but till today he never hit me and I think—don't laugh—he cares. I married him when he was riding high, now he's pretty low, makes me kind of a terrific fella to do that. That's what Duke would think anyway and I'm not sure he's wrong."

"Can I say something?"

"You can shut up, please, I'm doing my best. Okay. You: talented and terrific and on the come and listen, it wasn't just that for a second there our thoughts touched like you said it happened with your Merlin and his wife, that was important, sure, but the truth is, I don't know a whole lot in this world but if you don't love me, I don't know anything. Question: for how long? Answer: none possible. Problem: what if it stops."

"It won't."

"*You can't know that.* People change when they get famous and no doubt about it, you're gonna get famous and I'm not fifteen anymore, Corky, you think I am but I'm twice that and my breasts are starting to sag."

"I can prove otherwise with my own hands."

"You don't see *me,* that's the damn point. You see her, Peggy the cheerleader; well what happens when that stops? Don't say 'it won't stop,' I'm working to my climax.

"Okay. It crossed my mind during my endless driving that here's the situation: Duke's not perfect and you're maybe not gonna be perfect either. But then it hit me: *I'm miserable anyway,* Corky. So why should I stick around, it's my life. I'm taking off."

"With me, right?"

"Get this please: I'm leaving, and you're leaving, so it *happens* we'll go together but I'm not running out on Duke because *he's* at the bottom, I'm going because *I'm* at the bottom, so it happens by coincidence that you and I are heading the same direction, out, and if it works that we stay headed that same direction, terrific, but if it doesn't, the world's not ending for me, which is what I was afraid of, going off and leaving one guy and then getting dumped by another and not having the first one around to take me back but that's no problem, not anymore, 'cause if I get dumped, I'm not coming back."

Corky blinked. "My God, you mean I win?"

"If I'm a prize, then you're the winner." She leaned back wearily, closed her eyes. "And as soon as I finish explaining all this to Duke, we can take off . . ."

14

"Gee," Corky said, "do you think you ought to put yourself through all that?"

"I owe him that much."

"But you're tired, you know you are. I think you're just letting yourself in for a real emotional bloodbath. Call him when we're settled somewhere decent. Or write him a long letter; that's what I'd do."

She looked at him. "I've done dumb things all my life, not faced up to stuff. Today's about the hardest day I ever had but I feel really good about it, Corky. I've got to make Duke understand this—for my own good as well as his pride. He's got to know he didn't get dumped for another guy. *We failed together.* He's got to hear that from me." She looked at her watch. "He'll be home soon, it's getting dark, you can't hunt a whole lot when that happens."

"I wish you'd let me convince you I was right."

She went into his arms, held him a moment. "You go on back to the cabin and get ready. I'll pack too. He'll come in and we'll talk and then I'll come get you and g'bye."

"Hello," Corky said, and kissed her.

She kissed him back, then broke it. "Go on now. Please." He started for the door. "How come the Rolls-Royce people never showed?"

Corky smiled at her. "That was gonna be my surprise. I called the Postman when you were gone and said could he cancel them and would he trust me to take the car awhile—"

"And he said *yes?*"

"He's awful fond of me. He's only charging me fifty cents a mile."

Peggy started laughing. "Peggy Snow riding off into the sunset with a man who loves her *and* an eighty-thousand-dollar car." She sighed. "Into each life some rain must fall."

"I love you," he called as she started upstairs.

"You better, you bastard." He waved from the front door, left, closing it behind him.

"What was all that about?" Fats asked when Corky got back to the cabin.

"Nothing important. Just the future."

"And. *And?*"

Corky got his suitcase out of the closet.

"She's leaving him?" Fats cried out. "Fantastic."

Corky made a little bow.

"Unbefuckinglievable."

"You think I'm not a little shaky?"

"So what now?"

"I figure we kind of tool off in the Rolls and get to know each other some."

"Where though—where are we going?"

"Don't get emotional, but I was kind of wondering if you'd mind if it was just a honeymoon for two."

"What's the punch line?"

"Dead serious."

"You mean *leave* me behind?"

"I asked you not to get emotional. I just think it wouldn't hurt for me and Peg to get to know each other alone."

"You drive a hot white Corniche around you'll get to know the inside of a jail cell, period. You can't go without me, Cork —Jesus, who'll do your thinking—admit it, you hadn't figured that about the stolen car."

Corky shrugged, started packing. "So I'll dump it somewhere in a couple of days, big deal. No one's looking for it now. I'll leave it in a nice slum area, believe me, someone'll find a use for it and Peg and I will be long gone. I want to show her Paris."

"You sound like MauricefuckingChevalier—you've never been to Paris yourself, schmucko—what is this 'show her' routine?"

"I just want to be with her. The rest of the world can take care of itself."

"Hey, you're serious."

Corky nodded.

"Aw come on, Corky, this is me."

"I know. Don't think this is easy."

"Then why are you doing it at all?"

Corky sighed. "Because, frankly, there've been times when you've been almost too strong for me. You're a very imposing force and it's scary—I want to try getting a little objectivity."

"You don't dare leave me."

"Please don't make this terrible."

"I'll tell—I swear—in the middle of the act some night when you don't expect it I'll tell every goddam thing you've done up here—I mean it, Corky—"

Quietly, Corky said, "I don't think so."

"What makes you so goddam confident?"

"Because I'm doing a single from now on."

Fats didn't say anything.

"I think I've got the confidence to try it now. Peggy gives that to me. I did some coin stuff for her that was really charming. It's her, Fats. That's what she can do for me. I'm going to grab it while I can."

"You want me to beg?"

"Don't go on—"

"—Christ, kid, remember where you were before I came on the scene? *The gas was on.*"

". . . I know . . ."

"You're killing me, you know that?—I saved you—I was present at the creation—you just can't dump me now that you're on top—"

"I'm not on top—I've always bombed without you before, maybe I will again, all I'm saying is I want to try."

"Hey Cork . . . puh . . . please . . . keep me around at least . . . I can help . . . throw in a few lines maybe now and then . . . that's not something you can't live with . . ."

Corky kept on packing.

". . . I'm praying . . . please God change your mind . . .

please God say okay, Fats, you can tag along . . . please . . ."

Corky shook his head.

"Christ, do you know what loneliness is?"

Corky looked at Fats and nodded. "I been there myself," Corky said. "But no more . . ."

An hour later Peg came knocking. "I don't understand. I'm packed, I'm ready, I've practiced my speech till *I'm* getting bored with it, where is he?"

"Maybe he just hiked a long way and it's taking longer to get back than you figured."

"Possible." She nodded. "Usually he just tromps around this area but sometimes not."

"I really feel more strongly than ever that you're facing something you don't have to face. Be better for us all if we were gone."

Peg shook her head. "It's gotta be my way. But . . ." She stopped.

Corky looked at her to go on.

"I don't like waiting up there alone, too many memories, kind of scary almost, you mind if I stay down here till he comes?"

"Oh yeah," Corky said smiling. "I'd mind that like anything."

"And in honor of your stay with us," Fats said, "I'd like to sing a little song of my own composition. It's called, 'Duke.'

> 'Duke is a spook
> Who makes some of us puke
> But I won't sing no more
> 'Cause I ain't got my uke.'"

"Not one of your better efforts," Corky told him.

"Just trying to help little Peggy pass the time."

"I just hope he's not out drinking somewhere."

"There a bar around here?"

"No, but twice last year about this time he went out and he met a couple of other hunters and they had their car and went into Normandy and Duke didn't come rolling in till one in the morning."

"What time is it now?" Fats asked.

"Not even six," Peggy told him.

Fats did his Bette Davis. "Fasten your seat belts everybody; it's going to be a bumpy night."

"Who was that supposed to be?"

"That sound you heard was my ego breaking," Fats said. "That was Ezio Pinza, my dear."

Peggy broke out laughing.

"Don't encourage him," Corky said.

"Okay, all right, I can tell when I'm not appreciated, I just locked my mouth and threw away the key."

"Thank God for huge favors," Corky said.

Peggy got up, looked out a window across the lake. "Did he take a flash along, did you notice?"

"All I noticed was the elephant gun he was carrying—it was probably a peashooter but it looked mighty convincing to me. He just indicated like I said, that maybe it would be pleasing to all concerned for me to consider vacating the premises. And if he'd just get back, would I ever vacate."

"He can't be *much* longer," Peggy said. "Patience above all things." She sat down at the desk. Corky took the chair. They waited.

At six-thirty Peggy wondered if she should start to worry. Corky said that was up to her.

At seven Peggy said should she call the cops do you think. Corky said he thought she should call the bars. Peggy decided to hell with it.

But she was tensing.

"God*dammi*t," she said at seven-thirty.

"Well let's get the hell *out*," Corky answered.

"*No.*"

"It's *senseless* just waiting—"

"I'm *aware* of your opinion, Corky, you don't have to say it again—"

"—a little *common sense* never hurt, Peggy."

"Ahh, sweet mystery of life at last I've found you," Fats

blasted. "AHHHHHHHHHH at last I know the meaning of it all."

"I thought you were locked," Corky said.

"Well *somebody's* got to rescue you two from yourselves."

"And you're a guaranteed ray of sunshine, is that it?" Corky said.

"Well I don't want to brag, schmucko, but they didn't make me social director at Devil's Island for nothing."

"Not so good," Corky said.

"I could always sing my 'Duke' song again."

"Spare us," Peggy said.

"You're a tough house but—wait—wait—I've got it, we'll have a Vera Hruba Ralston festival—no, nuts, I forgot my projector."

Peggy started smiling. "God she was terrible. My mother was a movie freak—she even named me after Peggy Ann Garner."

"I didn't know that," Corky said.

"Well my God, you guys are just beginning with each other —Peg probably doesn't know you save your toenails—he does— fabulous collection—he's been written up in *Nails Unlimited*— that's kind of the bible of the toenail crowd—it's a minor subculture, like *Star Trek* freaks and people who keep Ring Ding wrappers." He looked at the two of them. "Things are warming up a little, right, right?"

"Some," Corky admitted.

Fats said to Peg, "Get Corky's cards, I'll read your fortune."

"Does Corky have cards here?"

"Does a bear evacuate in the woods?—notice how I'm toning up my language?—I got to, the Pope's hot for me to play the Vatican next Holy Week and I don't want the Pontiff getting pissed at me." Peggy laughed. "In the case. There should be half a dozen decks."

"I need to keep in practice," Corky said as Peg brought back several decks of cards.

"Security blankets and you know it, schmucko." Peg held out the cards. "Give me a hand," Fats said, and Corky came up and helped.

"Spread the cards," Fats said, "so I can concentrate."

Corky fanned with one hand.

"Hmmm," Fats said, studying the cards. "The cards tell all."

"Like what?" Peg asked.

Fats shut his eyes. "Your name . . . is . . . it's coming through clearly, yes, your name is Peggy Ann Blow—oops—"

"The Pope's gonna love slips like that," Corky said.

Fats looked at the cards again. "Snow, and you're—the sex is coming now—a *woman*."

"Most definitely," Corky said.

"And you're scared," Fats went on, "about are you doing the right thing, going off with the king of the toenail hoarders but the cards say chances are pretty good because he is a drooler, true, but an honest one, and you are a lady who digs honesty so all in all I would say if you can teach him to take a bath once a week whether he needs it or not, you got as good a shot as anyone of walking off into the sunset together."

"Thank you," Peggy said softly.

"Enough treacle," Fats said. "Corky, entertain us, make a little magic."

Corky shook his head. "Not in the mood."

"All right, *I'll* do it then."

"You do magic too?" Peg asked.

Fats shook his head. "Corky does magic, I can only do tricks, self-working stuff mostly, the garbage end of the leger-demain business. How'll I start? Hmmm." He closed one eye, tilted his head, paused. Then he said, "What the hell, let's start with a You Do as I Do."

"A *what?*" from Peg.

"Time passers is all, a series of tricks all with the same basic gimmick, they work great if you don't know, once you do they're a yawn."

"Show me."

"You want the patter or just the trick?"

"Whatever."

"The bare bones are kind of nothing, you take two decks and shuffle them separately and then you pick a card from

one of the decks and cut the cards and hand me that deck and
you take mine and find your card and I take yours and pull
the *same* card from your deck."

"That's not a trick," Peg said.

"It is, believe me," Fats began—

"—*it is not a trick*—"

"You're gonna make me give away the gimmick, you keep
on like that," Fats told her.

"Magic," Peg said. She was starting to slump down.

"It's so simple you're gonna whoopse," Fats said. "See, the
whole secret is that when you shuffle I peek at the bottom
card of your deck when you're shuffling and then when you
pick a card well, you've put the card you picked on top and
complete the cut and that brings the bottom card which *I*
know on top of your card that *you* know so when you give me
your deck, all I have to do is find the card below the bottom
card and that's your card."

". . . lying . . ."

"I know you can't believe it," Fats said, "'cause it sounds
too dumb to fool anybody but Corky, he makes a big produc-
tion out of it sometimes, especially when he wants to fuck
some broad he's picked up and he gives a big spiel about how
they were meant for each other and he can read her mind and
usually the first time he suckers her in by missing and so when
he does it she thinks, my God, this is kismet, let's hit the sack,
you can't believe how much people want to believe in magic,
my God, Corky's fucked stews from coast to coast with that
one and . . ."

And then Peg stood and her determination to withstand attack had been so strong that when it crumbled, there was
nothing left behind it, no defense, so the hysteria came fast
and her face fell apart and she spun for the door and was
halfway up the hill before Corky could grab her but she was a
powerhouse by then and he couldn't keep hold, and he
couldn't get a word in at the door of the main house and he
couldn't hold her tightly enough in his arms on the stairs and
when she locked herself in the bedroom he pounded, pleading
till his hands bruised but she was weeping far too out of con-

trol to hear or care or understand and when Corky finally realized she would not let him in, would never let him in, he found his way back to the cabin and Fats was staring at him as he entered and before Corky could get a word in Fats was screaming, *"That was just the beginning"* loud and clear.

Corky shook his head. "That was the end."

"I don't think so."

"I would have left you nice before. Comfortable. A warm place, decent, safe. Now I don't care if the cat gets your eyes."

"Listen to him."

"Done talking."

"Hear me out."

"Sorry."

"You've got to hear me."

"Make it fast."

"I will, I will, more Jesus, but don't stand hovering like the Frankenstein monster, sit down."

"No more jokes either," Corky said, as he sat in the desk chair. Fats was in the overstuffed one, eyes wide open.

"Why do you think I blew the whistle?"

"To cause pain."

"That's not the main reason though, why else?"

"Because you were jealous. Because I was leaving you. You were angry. Want me to go on?"

"You're missing why I did it."

"Educate me then."

"You ready?"

"Ready as I'll ever be."

"It's a lulu."

"Hit me, I'm braced."

"I DID IT BECAUSE I COULD."

Corky blinked.

Fats started laughing. "You don't get it yet, do you?"

Corky shook his head.

"WHY DIDN'T YOU STOP ME?"

Corky just waited.

"YOU DIDN'T BECAUSE YOU COULDN'T." Fats was roaring now. "He still doesn't get it. He's such a major league dimfuckingwit numskull he's sitting there and he doesn't understand. Remember a little ago when you were dumping me you said I was a very imposing force and it's scary? You said there were times when I was almost too strong for you? Schmucko, I've been too strong all along, all those stupid goddam wisdoms you helped me hunt and peck, 'I'm worried about Corky' 'Corky's afraid of success' 'What happens to all those girls Corky sees only once,' you thought you were faking me when it was ass-backwards, I was faking you."

"You got your rocks off now?"

"Not quite. I laid low, kept the quiet profile, things were going good enough, I don't mind a little limelight sharing when there's common gain, but then tonight, when I *begged* you, when I *humbled* myself and you said tough buddy, I'm out for number one now, well, that tore it. *Where was she when the gas was on?* I took a nothing, a technical whiz with the charm of Dick Nixon and I created a dazzler. And no two-bit hunk is gonna come along and ladle off the cream. It's you and me, not you and her, only from now on, it's gonna be me and you."

"Think it's maybe time to change the record?"

"If you're bored sitting there, by all means walk around."

Corky started pacing.

"Go in and splash some water on your face, maybe that'll help arouse your interest."

Corky went in to the sink, turned on the cold spigot, splashed some water on his face. When he came back out, Fats was laughing. "I must have missed the joke."

"You *are* the joke."

"You're too fast for the room I guess."

Fats was laughing so hard now it was hard for him to get the words out. "Those tricks—the ones we told Peggy about, those are called You Do as I Do."

"Well?"

"You could call *our* trick You Do as I Say. Sit down, Corky."

"I don't feel like it."

"Have a chair, keed."

Corky sat in the desk chair.

"Yawn."

"I'm not tired."

"Sure y'are."

Corky yawned, and stretched.

"Attaboy. Crawl."

Corky started crawling around the floor.

"Imitate me."

"Hey this is fanfuckingtastic," Corky said.

"Up and at 'em."

Corky jumped to his feet.

Fats picked up the rhythm—"Okay skip, okay hop, okay spin around, okay touch the ceiling, touch the floor, Fats says giggle, Fats says stop," and Corky, after skipping and spinning and giggling stood there catching his breath.

"Believe me now, schmucko?"

Corky nodded.

"It's our secret, yours and mine. I'll handle it smooth in public, we'll never let on. And then in private, I'll have my little games like this just to remind you that it was a little bit of a boo-boo when you decided to dump me for the broad."

Corky continued to breathe heavily.

"You can talk now, say whatever you want, as long as I want you to, when I'm bored, we'll play some more."

"Lis—"

"—I'm bored, let's play, get the knives."

"Knives?"

"The Duker's, go get 'em."

Corky went to the kitchenette, brought out the knives.

"What do you think we ought to do with 'em?" Fats said.

"Want me to whittle something?"

"Maybe."

"I'm very fast. I can make things in a flash. Really."

"I'm looking for something with a little more pizzazz."

Corky just stood there waiting.

Fats had to laugh. "What is that whittling shit? Trying to

fake me out? Those days is gone, schmucko. I'm with you every step of the way. Now. Tell me. What do you think we ought to do with those nice sharp knives of old Duke's?"

"Don't," Corky said.

"I don't feel any passion in your tone yet."

"Please don't kill her."

"I would never deprive you of that pleasure, you think I'm cruel or something?"

"I can't."

"I got faith in you."

"She won't let me in. The door's locked. It's thick. I can't break it down."

"You'll use the old noggin. I'm just gonna wait down here nice and comfy and then when you get back, you can tell me all about it."

"I WON'T."

"How's your head, Cork?"

"My head?"

"Yeah. I think you're getting yourself a little migraine."

"No. I'm not." But his left eye was starting to blink.

"Feels like it could be a bad one. One of those gut wrenchers that can go on for days."

Corky's hands went to his eye, pressed hard.

"Drop your hands."

Corky put his hands down.

"It's getting bad fast, Cork, I can tell. You're losing color."

"Please stop it."

"It's really drilling deep, isn't it?"

"Yes. Yes."

"Surprise!"

Corky stopped blinking.

"Going away now?"

Corky nodded.

"Not deep at all, right? Almost gone?"

Nod.

"Totally gone?"

Nod.

"Want it back? Want it back a hundred times worse, *a hundred times worse and a hundred days long?* Yes?"

Shake.

"Then get a wiggle on."

Corky put the knives in his back trouser pockets, started for the door.

"And do it beautifully," Fats called.

15

"Duke?" Peggy called when the knock came. She was lying across the bed, tears past, past tears, empty.

"Me."

Peggy stared at the ceiling.

"I left schmucko down at the cabin. I had to talk to you Peg, open the door, huh?"

". . . Duke doesn't want you here when he gets back, that goes for me now . . ."

"Duke's got nothing against me. He laughed at me at breakfast."

". . . I mean it, Corky . . ."

"I told you, he's down at the cabin, we're the only ones that can straighten this out, Peg. That's why I came up alone."

To her amazement, Peg started to cry again. Funny; she didn't think there were any left.

"I've got a present that'll make you smile."

". . . go 'way, Corky . . ."

"Fats."

". . . all right, go away, Fats."

"Well, at least that's done, at least we know who we are."

Peggy began wondering about Duke, pushing her mind to him, trying to figure how it might work out. They'd sell this place, get beans for it, but maybe enough for a camper, a trailer, something so they could live cheap. Head west maybe to Washington. The country was supposed to be beautiful. Rainy a lot, but—

"Don't you want my present, Peggy?"

"I don't want anything, Fats."

". . . Peggy Ann Snow
Peggy Ann Snow

Please let me follow
Wherever you go . . ."

—but so what if it rained, she'd still have a roof over her head, a man—she groaned. The man would be Duke. Blowing in her ear forever.

"That's a little poem Corky made up about a jillion years ago. I wanna tell you something: it's kept him warm a lot. Please take his present. He made it for you to remember him by. He's leaving, Peg. But would you keep this thing?"

"What thing?"

"A heart. He whittled it for you before he sent me up here. It didn't take him long, he's quick with his hands—it's the second heart he made for you—the first was when he left in high school but he threw it away in case you laughed at it or something."

She was momentarily, goddammit, touched.

"I'll just say this last and then I'll go. The reason I told about the mind reading. Corky was too embarrassed to tell you himself. I lied when I said he'd done it before, that was just to make it as bad as possible. He felt that crappy about himself. But, see, Cork hasn't got a lot of confidence and he did the mind reading because he didn't think anyone as perfect as you would look at him otherwise."

She said nothing but it was true; Corky was always running himself down.

"And Peg, he never thought you'd actually care for him. Then when you did and he'd lied, well, it killed him. It just destroyed him because you hate liars and he hates liars but for love he'd lied and he couldn't go off with you for the rest of his life with a lie at the foundation. So that's it. Would you take his heart, Peg? At least if you did, he'd know you understood and didn't feel contempt for him."

"Oh I never felt contempt."

"At least that's something."

"Leave it outside the door."

"You won't open it then?"

"Just leave it."

There was a pause. She heard something touch the bottom of the door. "G'bye."

Peg waited awhile before she said, "You didn't walk away."

"Brains as well as boobs."

Peg caught herself before she smiled.

"—he *needs* you, Peg. He did stuff for you he never did for anybody—the coins dancing around his fingers—he doesn't need me anymore—that's what you mean to him, you give him that much confidence, *now take the goddam heart or he'll die!*"

It was really stupid not to at least take it. She'd been talking, was there any difference really in talking to someone through a door or with it open? Who was she kidding? Take the heart, nod, say good-bye. She got off the bed, unlocked the door, opened it and was twice surprised. Once was how lovely the heart was.

But why were the knives in his hand . . . ?

Corky dropped the bloody knives on the overstuffed chair beside Fats. "Take a load off," Fats said.

Corky walked slowly to the sofa, sat.

"You seem a little glum, a bit morose, don't be, I got a piece of good news for you."

Corky only shrugged.

"A: I wanna apologize. I was too rough before. It had to be done, things had to be got shipfuckingshape fast, but all in all, I wasn't any too delicate and I'm sorry. But the biggie is this: I'm not gonna make you remember."

Corky nodded.

"I'd like a little more enthusiasm, please. My God, if I wanted to I could have you seeing her corpse and hearing her cry out and all that but I don't carry a grudge like some people, so I hereby give you my promise I won't let you remember. Say 'Thank you.'"

"Thank you."

"Now don't you feel better?"

Corky shook his head and started to cry. He stretched full out on the sofa and sobbed.

"—aw Laddie, come on now—"

"—please—"

"—don't go to pieces on me—"

Corky could not stop crying.

"All right, it's been a big day, get it out of your system."

Corky kept on sobbing.

"Wanna tell Fats about it?"

"She . . . liked the heart . . ."

"You're a great whittler, she damn well should have."

". . . I pleased her . . . no tricks . . . just me . . ."

"Sure, sure. Feeling a little more under control now?"

Corky nodded.

"Okay, good, pay attention now because I think it's time we did a little serious changing in the act, so let me hit you with a couple notions: what say we cut down on the magic and replace it with me doing a couple of snazzy musical numbers, say you like it."

"I like it."

"Good, I kind of had a feeling you would because . . . because . . ."

"What's wrong?"

"I don't know how to say this since I haven't got a stomach, but my stomach hurts."

"Bad?"

"Getting . . . bad."

Corky's arm slipped to the floor.

"Getting . . . real bad now . . ."

"Yes . . ."

". . . what—is this . . . ?"

". . . we're dying I think is what it is . . ."

". . . dying . . . ?"

". . . after I gave her the . . . heart . . . on my way back down . . . I put them deep in me . . ."

". . . Christ it's spreading . . . getting worse . . ."

". . . I know . . ."

". . . don't leave me here alone . . ."

". . . I would . . . never . . ."

". . . can you get over . . . ?"

Corky slowly used his arms, got across the floor. ". . . what now . . . ?"

". . . put me . . . flat . . ."

Corky did his best. ". . . help any . . . ?"

Fats lay on the soft chair cushion. ". . . I hope I don't go first is all . . ."

Corky had to close his eyes. ". . . Fats . . . ?"

". . . right here, Laddie . . ."

". . . she really liked my heart . . ."

". . . why didn't you . . . take off with her then . . . ? you had control . . . why didn't you just go . . . ?"

". . . cuz . . . she would never have left with me . . . I couldn't face failure again . . . see, I couldn't even make her open the door alone . . . it was never me . . . always us . . ."

". . . schmucko . . . us was you . . ."

". . . huh . . . ?"

". . . it was you all the time . . ."

". . . you sure . . . ?"

". . . trust me for a while . . ."

16

Peggy lay on the bed for a long time and studied the lovely wooden heart. God he had wonderful hands. She stayed on the bed, turning the heart over and over. Then she got up and examined herself in the mirror. She looked fifty easy, what with the puffy eyes and the wrinkled clothes, but a change of wardrobe could fix the one, Max Factor could go a long way toward helping with the other. When she was pretty again, she put on a nice dress because even though she didn't love him, Corky's kind of talent you had to string along with, and with that thought firmly in mind, she went down to the cabin to tell him so . . .